RESCUING AVA

RESCUING AVA

Vivien Varga

Copyright © 2024 Vivien Varga

The moral right of the author has been asserted.

Apart from any fair dealing for the purposes of research or private study, or criticism or review, as permitted under the Copyright, Designs and Patents Act 1988, this publication may only be reproduced, stored or transmitted, in any form or by any means, with the prior permission in writing of the publishers, or in the case of reprographic reproduction in accordance with the terms of licences issued by the Copyright Licensing Agency. Enquiries concerning reproduction outside those terms should be sent to the publishers.

This is a work of fiction. Names, characters, businesses, places, events and incidents are either the products of the author's imagination or used in a fictitious manner. Any resemblance to actual persons, living or dead, or actual events is purely coincidental.

Troubador Publishing Ltd
Unit E2 Airfield Business Park,
Harrison Road, Market Harborough,
Leicestershire LE16 7UL
Tel: 0116 279 2299
Email: books@troubador.co.uk
Web: www.troubador.co.uk

ISBN 978-1-83628-040-8

British Library Cataloguing in Publication Data.
A catalogue record for this book is available from the British Library.

Printed and bound in the UK by TJ Books Limited, Padstow, Cornwall
Typeset in 12pt Minion Pro by Troubador Publishing Ltd, Leicester, UK

*For my family and friends,
with love x*

Several Years Later

'Escaping Entrapment.'
By Isla Mills

Beatrice had learnt, only now, to distance and ignore the malefic, spiteful beings whose sole purpose seemed to be to seek out and disturb the peace of others. These days she could shrug off their salt-sour, scorn-veiled mannerisms, icy expressions, and alienate the festering venom crouching thirstily in wait behind their ugly utterances. She was able to deftly distance their 'like butter wouldn't melt' comments, laced with strychnine, which had, once upon a time, infected her innocent, open soul, stripped her of self-esteem and thrust her into a dark, dark corner... but not now.

Now she understood her predators for who they really were. Observed from above, oh so far above, in her calm mind, their deep-seated inadequacy, jealousy, spite; and thus, with kind... yes, kind, wise eyes, she silently slid back through mid-air the poisonous strands of arrowed abuse, while sagely noting the false, acrid smirks of these lamentable brutes transform into marked, and real, displeasure that their attack had *been thwarted, leaving their smug faces to transmute into grimacing gargoyles.*

And although many a long year had passed prior to her finally acquiring this freedom, she was now able to shed the heinously burdensome baggage, the age-old anguish, thus casting it ceremoniously into a deep, metal, Pandoran casket, firmly secured by heavy nails, before posting it to the cavernous ash heap of history, forever lost in Hadean depths, never to rear its hateful head again.

Following her liberation, her proficiency at tolerating from afar, even pitying, these poor, pathetic creatures with their malicious intentions cruelly residing, unchanged, behind cold, featureless masks, was commendable. What a shame, she would muse patiently, perceptively: poor them! Yes, she could even stretch to generosity from her new standpoint of knowledge... of power!

But once upon a time...

Present

Aunt Pam's Visit

Frayed nerves flickered uneasily as Isla fixed an anxious gaze on the window, dreading their imminent arrival. And all too soon, her rapidly mounting tension was to further intensify as the sudden brash glare of harsh headlights cut through the glass, cruelly flooding the softness of the sitting room like a searchlight, leaving her nowhere to hide. A tiny, fragile moth with light-brown tissue-paper wings veered feather-like, helplessly treading air in a desperate bid to swerve to safety... like her pulsing heart, which rose and sank inside her chest, causing her breath to race.

"They're here, Isla, look sharp. Open the door, will you. Don't keep them waiting." Her father's voice was terse and rigid.

Answering his command, her faint (from jumping up too quickly), fraught frame fluttered towards the bright light as, with shaking hands, she turned the door handle. No escape now.

The slate-grey, predatory eyes of her hateful aunt (*great* aunt, to be exact), taut-skinned (due to Botox and her latest face-lift), lay in judgement, forcing the child to blink and shift awkwardly from one foot to the other. Her uncle, Clive, slicked-back pewter hair set hard like granite, nodded, his detachment visible despite a slight, swift smile.

"Hello, Aunt," she managed. "Uncle."

"Goodness, child, what have you been eating?" Aunt Pam scanned her niece scathingly. "Surely not that dreadful processed chicken your mother serves up! You need fresh food in you, vegetables, fish, dear. That will improve your complexion and put a bit of weight on you. You're skin and bone, positively scrawny."

Isla shuffled, blankly nodding as her head pounded and sought to burst its banks. The constant references to her mother's failings tore unrelenting at her already restless soul.

"Get me some tea, child, in your china cups, not those ghastly thick mugs your mother bought years ago."

Again the girl nodded and, relieved to escape, fled to the kitchen, inadvertently clenching her teeth. She wanted to spit into the hot, dark liquid and pour it over her aunt's lap. Yes, she did, but instead, delivered it silently to the low, angular table positioned in humble subservience in front of the thankless woman.

"Hello, Pam. How are you? Glad you could make it." Her father appeared from behind the dark wood door, an affable grin now rearranging the contours of his previously taut lips.

"Good afternoon, Peter," came the cordial reply, and as they retired to the lounge, the stringy vein on his aunt's neck twitched reflexively; and her jet-black hair, tightly set with a couple of curled coils, like poodle pelt, stuck fast to her shiny forehead – a feature which, purely created to detract from her overly pointed nose, fell vastly short of its remit!

And now seated bolt-upright on a wood-framed armchair, Isla remained motionless, only managing to endure tedious adult conversation by disappearing into her inner space, where she peered at the ornately floral rug and envisaged her mother cross-legged on the floor, laughing, joking with her as they traced the pale pink flowers in this silky indoor meadow. She could see her soft, wavy hair and bright eyes, full of life, a world away from a month ago, when a dull, glassy stare caught her frightened gaze as they took her mother away.

"How is your schoolwork coming along?" Her aunt brusquely interrupted her quietude, thus jolting her back to reality.

"Um… fine, thank you," she replied, not choosing to elaborate.

"*Well…* are you getting top grades?" the now-agitated woman persisted.

"In some subjects."

"You should be achieving top marks in everything, Isla dear, not just *some subjects*. Work harder in future, child, if you wish to succeed."

"Yes, Aunt."

"Let's make our way to the dining room," suggested

Father after what seemed an eternity. "I do hope you like venison."

"Yes, more than tolerable. Where is your mother?" Aunt Pam focused exclusively on Isla before selecting her seat at the head of the dark wood table.

"Sh… she was called away… an emergency." The child stared at her shoes.

"Really? She was absent on our last visit too, and the one before that." The reply was cold like the sorbet dessert.

"It was unavoidable," added Isla's father awkwardly. "Last minute. She sends her apologies."

"Yes, I bet she does." And silence claimed the room.

Isla's aching shoulders sank, and she felt limp like a collapsed marionette.

The evening dragged dreadfully, dreary dialogue hung dully in the air, and she longed to break away from this miserable place.

It was much later, when the clock struck ten, that her father declared abruptly: "Time for bed." And even though his tone was dismissive, Isla thanked God for this welcome release and, quietly bidding goodnight to the awful guests, she gratefully retired to the heaven-sent sanctum of her bedroom.

Her mother was in hospital. She had been there for one month – a psychiatric unit in the hills. Father had, as yet, deemed it unnecessary to reveal this to his relatives as it was, in his words: 'a private affair', which, translated, meant 'shameful' and 'embarrassing'. So, due to this decision, the same charade had to be played out every time his aunt and uncle visited.

Isla longed to scream: *"It's your fault* – all of you, with your aloof, controlling behaviour, your constant disapproval – *your fault*, you drove her to it – all of you!" But she said nothing.

On drawing back the flimsy net drapes, which had captured several hapless flies in their folds, she observed the sharp white moon, clear, confident, intense, in the deep, dark, distant sky… and breathed in; its massive majesty momentarily set her free, and her aunt, for a while at least, faded to a tiny, insignificant dot.

Past

Sing a Happy Song While You Can

"Dance, girl, show him how it's done. He can't take his eyes off you. I do believe he's drooling!"

"That's gross, Jen! Just leave it out! You're making me feel self-conscious!"

"*You, self-conscious!* Ha, that's a laugh. Since when exactly?"

"I'm going to get drinks. Do you want a refill?"

"Yeah, go on then. Why not."

Battling through the dense, sweaty bodies, which manically vied for precious space on the slippery, cocktail-sticky dance floor, Ava, exuding radiance in her gold-sequined mini-dress, eventually reached the brightly lit bar, where swarms of fresh-faced youths swung on pink leather stools or leant heavily on the now smeary, stained glass counter, abuzz with raucous laughter and animated discourse.

It was here she met the man. The man who had been watching her. The man who changed her life.

"The dancing queen," he remarked, having followed her to the bar. And their eyes met.

She smiled fleetingly, while attempting to catch the barwoman's attention.

"I was watching you," he declared, casually adding, "but not in an untoward way, of course. Just admiring your moves."

"Two gin and tonics, please. So, no voyeuristic tendencies. That's a relief." She feigned indifference, while noting his dark eyes and open charm. "Well, nice meeting you." With drinks precariously balanced in each hand and doubting her chances of ever negotiating her way back through the dizzy throngs, Ava, nevertheless, turned to face the imminent challenge.

"Wait, let me help you." The silver-tongued words which emerged resolutely from the stranger caused her to instantly reconsider her prior intentions, and – "Thanks," she said, somewhat relieved.

Reaching out assertively, the man grasped the drinks before leading the way back to the dance floor.

And this was her first mistake… the first of many.

Present

Oh Miseria, Let Me Be

Dawn and the net curtains shrouded the window like lost dreams, their thin light threads, falling rain. Isla sighed. They would all be seated in the breakfast room by 8am. And, curling up as compact as a sleeping kitten under the starched covers, she silently sought solace in her private place before having to weather the looming storm, where her mouth would force tight smiles and her words be born fractured and faint.

A feeble meow drifted in from the garden as the cat, Marmalade – her mother's cat, her cat, who had been cruelly turfed outside in the cold again – was complaining. Father's orders had dictated its demeaning fall from grace, which had come to pass, in fact, solely due to Aunt Pam's hatred of animals, all animals, which she deemed 'loathsome and unclean'; so when she visited, the sorry creature, much against its will, was forced to take residence in the rotting ruins of a long-forsaken garden shed, which hugged a nearby stone wall for crucial comfort and support.

In thick woollen socks, the child slid to the full-length mirror and stared at her reflection – '*scrawny*', her aunt had said. She scrutinised her stick-thin frame, still visible in the oversized dressing-gown, and exhaled. Her solemn, dark eyes peered critically at the pasty complexion before her, and she thought that maybe her aunt had been right after all. What a sad specimen she appeared to have become. And an empty gloom trickled through her, like previously unshed tears, ending its solitary journey just inside her tired heart.

Past

Beware the Venus Fly Trap

"This is my friend, Jennifer," she said by way of introduction. "And I'm Ava."

"Peter," he replied, placing the drinks on one of the round, smoked-glass tables, which hugged the dance floor. "Nice to officially meet you."

"Do you want to dance?" invited Jen, her laughter infectious, as she flew onto the light-drenched space, whirling like a frenzied pole dancer.

"No. I'll just sit for now," came the clipped, cold response.

"Me too," agreed Ava, unaware of his dismissive tone, as she sat down to sip her gin.

Talk turned to work. She was an artist and had sold several of her paintings to small galleries, which provided her with a suitable income. He was an investment banker, which was met with an awkward pause, before she commented, "Oh, that's nice. Sounds impressive."

Funny, they only rarely talked about his profession in years to come, yet hers was visited frequently.

"Why don't you give it up and earn some decent money? You're not good enough to sell to top-end galleries, so what's the point? You're covered in paint every day, like a pre-school toddler, and the attic room – or 'studio', as you like to call it – could, almost certainly, be put to better use."

And she would stand statue-still, a dull pain quietly pulsing in her breast.

As the evening drew to a close, they exchanged numbers, promising to meet up for a coffee the following week. And he bade her goodbye before striding away, his gait self-assured, unwavering.

"I'm not certain about him," said Jennifer, wrinkling her nose in disapproval once he had exited the venue. "Seems a bit aloof. Did you see how he looked at me, with those stony eyes, when I asked him to dance? He was positively frosty, verging on churlish."

"I didn't notice," replied Ava, staring at his phone number written on a gilt-framed business card. "He seems sweet. And handsome, you've got to admit."

"Well, if you say so, but be very careful and watch yourself. Don't rush into anything."

"Wow! OK, Mum." And she placed the phone number securely in her purse.

Mistake number two.

Present

Finding a Voice

The laser-steel rain, which shot like bullets to the sodden ground, was gently daubed by the early morning sun in a fragile, straw-yellow glow, providing this drab, depressing scene with a warm, albeit weak, optimism. Yet, as she looked on, Isla knew the envious, grey clouds would soon sweep grudgingly across it, thus obliterating its peaceful rays of hope. And, forlornly, she sank back into the darkness of her room.

What should she wear? Anything she chose would, without a doubt, be scrutinised with acutely critical eyes, inducing her to wish she could merge, unobserved, into the wallpaper. After trying on an array of garments, she decided on a pale-yellow blouse, her mother's favourite, and jeans – breakfast time was, after all, less formal. And, satisfied she had selected well, she walked with relative composure down the stairs and into the conservatory which adjoined the kitchen.

"Good morning, Aunt, Uncle," she said as she made her way to the table. "Father."

"Morning, Isla, sit here," ordered her father, indicating a nearby chair.

"Goodness, child, what are you wearing?" exclaimed her aunt before the girl had time to take a seat. "That pale top must surely have seen better days, it's washed out, dear – and *jeans*? Just like a boy. What were you thinking?"

"She looks more like a boy," offered Uncle helpfully, as he cracked his egg.

Isla remained silent, hurriedly spooning cereal into her bowl, followed by a dash of milk; actions which provided an ordered distraction from the unkind words. But her entire body shook involuntarily, and her father noticed.

"Go. Put on a cardigan and a skirt. If you'd have been dressed properly in the first place, you wouldn't be shivering." His hard voice reached her like a sharp slap, and humiliated, she rushed to the door, eyes focused firmly on the floor.

Once out of view, and unable to further hide all the harboured hurt, she allowed hot tears to escape in a flush of anger and hatred, leaving her drained and downcast. Then, woodenly, she dressed and returned to the table.

"That's better. More ladylike. Where did you buy the cardigan?"

"From the boutique in the local shopping centre." Her reply was flat and lifeless.

"Yes, they do have reasonably priced clothes there," continued her aunt. "Not excellent quality, but perfectly acceptable if one wishes to dress *down*." And she chewed with feigned approval on the last word as if masticating gristly meat.

"Another boiled egg, Pam?" asked Father.

"No, we'll have to be heading off soon if we're to be back for our luncheon date."

And within the hour, the dreadful guests were gone. Their car had rolled heavily down the drive, and, barely able to conceal her elation, Isla let out a huge sigh of relief and waved them off with inflated cheer, her head brimming with emotion like the vigour and gusto of a million-pound lottery winner.

But now, standing in the big, empty hall, her short-lived contentment dissolved as she glanced at her father. If she didn't pluck up the courage to finally ask the question which had been tormenting her for too long, she never would.

He was, however, one step ahead.

"I have some work to do," he stated firmly. "What are your plans for the day? Any homework?"

"Um… no, I've done it."

"Well, you can revise for your end of term exams then."

She stood, hopelessly searching for her voice. *Come on, say it, say it!*

"I… I want to see Mother." The words were quiet but resolute and she waited with bated breath for his response.

"Not possible, Isla; your mother will be drugged up to the eyeballs, she probably won't even know who you are. It's not a good idea. So, go to your room and use the rest of the day productively." And, somewhat irritated, he strode purposefully towards the study, leaving Isla rooted to the spot like a neglected houseplant.

The recently maligned feline was immediately readmitted into the warm; and now mollified, lost no time in eagerly following the distraught child upstairs to her bedroom. After a night of suffering *hellish* deprivation, it bounced exuberantly onto the cosy bed, in pursuit of – like her – much needed affection. And squeezing into her outstretched arms, it purred compassion as its soft, silky fur absorbed her silent tears.

Past

Swim Home, Little Fish, Swim Home

Chomping happily on a warmed croissant, Ava snuggled up on the cushioned sofa, and, with her mouth full of buttery sweetness, hummed contentedly to a song on the radio. Such was her comfort, that when the phone rang from the table, she very nearly didn't answer it, but decided, on reflection, to bother, just in case it was important.

"Hello? Yes, this is she... oh hi! Good to hear from you. Yeah, I'm free tonight... OK, that's fine. Sounds great. Where? Wow, that's a posh restaurant... beats a coffee! OK. Shall I meet you there at seven? Wonderful. See you soon. Bye."

"Did you eat all the croissants? You pig!" complained Jen, appearing from nowhere and sleepily slouching towards the table, her eyes adjusting to the bright sunshine leaking into the kitchen.

"You have Einstein hair," remarked Ava, her lips curling up in amusement. "And there's one croissant waiting in the microwave, so quit complaining. Oh – and guess what? I have a date!"

"Really? Oh God! Please tell me it isn't haughty Henry from the other night."

"He is not haughty, nor is he called Henry, as you well know! He's very sweet – and he's *only* taking me to that posh Italian restaurant in town."

"Oh, lucky you! I'd rather eat rotting kale and marmite in the landfill tip."

"Oh, please don't mince words, just say it as it is!"

"Look, I've told you what I think. So, prove me wrong and have a great time, but don't say I didn't warn you if it all goes pear-shaped and he turns out to be a psycho!"

What should she wear? Clearly something formal, but not too revealing. Maybe her long black dress? Or short red one? He would probably wear a suit, she thought, so maybe black… yes, that would be sufficiently chic to give a good impression. And, once the decision had been made, the best part of two hours was spent fussing over accessories; until, finally, she found herself sitting on the back seat of a taxi in a state of edgy excitement.

"It's just up this road, near the square," she explained nervously to the driver. "You can drop me here. Thanks."

The imposing door, with etched, opaque glass and a surround of exquisite mouldings, sat in state at the top of white, stone steps fringed with ornate railings; the height of each level prompted her instinctively to lift her skirt so as not to trip, and to chew her lower lip, a habit she had formed when feeling insecure as a child.

"Good evening, madam," the doorman drawled, while affectedly opening the heavy door, proud, and perhaps superior, in his brass-buttoned waist coat and white trousers. Surprising what a uniform can do.

Once inside, she propped herself awkwardly against the bar, eager for her date to surface, and fumbling with her small, pewter clutch bag, could not help but observe all the unflustered diners, laughing and at ease, with linen serviettes and silver forks perfectly placed, and animated dialogue flying confidently through rouged lips. Why, then, did she feel like this, a fish out of water? What was wrong with her? *Relax, girl, just chill*, came the inner mantra until she discerned, from afar, the sound of her name.

"Ava? Hello…? Ava. Nice to see you again. You were in another world." And assertively, Peter took her arm before leading her to a candle-lit table, where an array of crystal-clear glasses, like bubbles, and two white roses in a tall black vase decorated the perfectly pressed, white-linen tablecloth.

"I like your dress. Very formal," came his ironed grin. "We should go to a dancehall afterwards."

"Oh dear, is it too much?"

"No, it's fine. You look more mature than in the club."

As in older? Or had she appeared immature before? She wasn't sure how to react, so said nothing.

"What's your tipple?" he continued, comfy in his quarter-zipper, cashmere top.

"Oh, um… G and T, please."

"Maybe some white wine first. Goes well with the fish. Are you happy with that?"

"Oh… yes, great," she said, although it would have been nice to peruse the menu and choose for herself. *Why, then, didn't she say something?* Still, he obviously knew what he was talking about and was maybe even masking his *own* nervousness by being a tad overzealous.

An awkward pause ensued before he resumed.

"My aunt dines here regularly, so my choices follow her recommendations."

"Oh… your aunt."

"Yes, Pam, she works in antiques and owns a shop in Knightsbridge. My parents were killed in a car crash while driving to a business lunch; from then on, she looked after me. I was just five when it happened."

"How awful! Such a sad story. I'm so sorry."

"Well, it was a long time ago now. What about you?"

"Me? Um… well, my mum lives in Cornwall in a coastal cottage; it's beautiful down there. I'm not in contact with my father – my parents separated, and he left for a new life in Australia with a woman young enough to be his daughter – *and*, as you know, I paint. Currently, I share a flat with my best friend, Jen, whom you have already met, albeit briefly."

"Ah, yes, Jen – an extremely *lively* character. All very interesting. I'd love to come over and see your artwork sometime."

"Ha-ha, they're not etchings, you know, so don't get your hopes up."

They both laughed, and a buzz of relaxation flushed through her; the wine, she had to admit, had helped.

And, at the end of the evening, he ordered a taxi and kissed her lightly on the lips.

"Thanks for the meal."

"My pleasure. I'll be in touch," he said.

"Yes, I'd like that."

And the wheels were set in motion. Her third mistake.

Present

A Secret Sanctum

Isla would go for days on end without seeing her father. More often than not he was out with clients, colleagues and sometimes friends he had kept in touch with from school days. There were also several women in his life (had been for years), mostly casual contacts, and never did he bring any home. When he had one in tow, he seemed slightly more mellow, but none of his conquests lasted long – lucky for them!

It was 3am and the child was woken by a car door slamming hard and, shortly afterwards, a fumbling attempt at the key in the lock, followed by the ungainly entry of her father accompanied by a multitude of expletives as he teetered and tottered the entire length of the hallway before collapsing in an untidy heap at the foot of the stairwell.

Listening intently, Isla wondered if she should go to his aid, but this scenario was not an isolated one and she did not want to be sworn at; also, she was by no conceivable means strong enough to help him up the stairs, so she remained still and waited. And eventually, the ghoul-like body managed to stagger in the direction of the sofa where it flopped with a drunken groan. The brief period of quiet which ensued was soon to be followed by rasping, raucous snorts like the inexpert blasting of a discordant trumpet.

Satisfied he would be out for the night and by now wide awake, Isla, quiet as a dormouse, stole across the night-blessed landing and up a diminutive flight of rickety stairs to a humble wooden door; and carefully rotating the key her mother kept under the coir welcome mat, she entered the hidden haven, where colours of truth lay concealed, gently closing the door behind her.

The studio lights, when switched on, were of a warm orange with individual white lights shining directly above some of the paintings: the ones positioned on the few easels dotted around the edges of the snugly compact attic space. The remainder of the art pieces, mostly earlier ones, were leaning patiently one on the other against the cream-plaster wall. And cocooned in this sacred shrine, Isla raptly inhaled her mother's precious presence.

Gently waving the dust from the thick stack of canvases, she scrutinised each one closely, not wanting to waste a moment, overlook a tender brushstroke, a poignant dab of paint. The vibrant colours of these former pieces entreated, enticed, like the sparkling, bright lights of a funfair. Such happiness: balloons, bubbles, striking reds, turquoises, aquamarines, shimmering pinks…

curves, arcs which embraced, reached out, effortlessly connecting at every turn. Enchanting. Magical.

But gradually, her eyes were drawn to an imposing oil painting propped on a tripod and of a vastly different mould. Its thick black mount seemed to box-in, entrap the subject, namely an exquisite face fashioned in pale porcelain, which stared vacantly out at her, with a glazed, doll-like emptiness. And the perfectly smooth ivory complexion was laced in tiny, hairline cracks (like the craquelure on old works of art), which shrouded the entire visage in a fine web of clear silk strands. Unmoving and mesmerised, Isla fixed intently on the sorrowful image, only later noting the date and name scrawled thickly in black at the bottom, a far cry from the intensely delicate precision of the subject matter. And she realised with a stark shudder that this had been her mother's last painting, completed just a week before she had been taken away. Ava's final cry for help.

Isla curled up on the little rainbow rug in the centre of the room and closed her eyes… until she drifted… her head filling with red, turquoise, orange shades in sun-sprinkled, cloud-like bubbles, which slid, gliding, skimming the soft surface of clear-blue skies. Exhilaration filled her lungs… a heavenly peace.

"Look at me, Mum; look, I'm flying!" And far, far below, the yellow boats, dotted on the frolicking waves, chattered and nodded rapturously!

"Freedom, Isla, freedom." And the beautiful silver-winged goddess, lightly floating on her wispy throne, was Ava.

Swirling, spinning bubbles gyrated like tiny helicopter seeds through the warm breeze, swinging, whirling, twirling…

"I never want to come down, ever!" cried Isla. "Let's stay up here, in the heavens, forever free."

"You and me, forever free," echoed her mother. "Dream, my love, dream."

But through the calm raged a sudden storm, lashing from the heights, unleashing sharp needles of rain like shrapnel from above, and Isla was struck mercilessly by these callous metal shards, which pierced her soft, warm skin.

"Mum! Help! I'm falling… falling!"

The dark-grey gale, its angry face a sneering, deadly crow, swept over her, stubbing out all light, and her plaintive screams were forever lost in its rasping breath.

Sharp, pointed bullets of glassy hail chipped and cracked her mother's delicate, porcelain face. Ava was sinking, loose white feathers drifting, fading. Her bruised, blistered bubble burst, littering the sky with a splash of red, as a blue-black crow tore her flesh, leaving her terror-stricken visage, all hope gone, ploughing into greedily waiting, deep-black waters.

Feeble pleas beseeched the heavens, all too frail to wake the gods; while vultures flocked, orbiting, circling, inches away, rendering Isla motionless, benumbed, her screams silent.

"*Ahhhhh!*"

She jolted suddenly upright and shuddered. A cold sweat stuck to her shivering frame and slowly rising, she crept unsteadily across the hard floor, switched off the lights and closed the door, returning the key to its secret place, before slipping silently to her bedroom, where she slid beneath the ice-cold covers.

"*Isla, we're late! Where the hell are you?*" shouted her father, brutally cutting through her heavy, morning sleep. "You've got five minutes, then I'm leaving, and you can catch the bloody bus!"

"Coming," she called back, swiftly pulling on her uniform, splashing her face and belting downstairs, manically finger-combing unruly, scarecrow hair.

"Ready!" came her breathless declaration, as she dragged a carton of juice from the fridge, plucked an apple from the bowl and slung her rucksack over her shoulders.

Once in the car, however, and about to turn on the engine, her father was interrupted by a shrill, woeful screech of Highland bagpipes which was, lamentably, his chosen ringtone.

"God, I'm late as it is," he complained, but his irritation was soon to wane. "*Oh dear, Pam… yes, yes… so sorry… condolences. When? Yes, of course, I'll be right over. Give me half an hour. Hang in there. Bye for now.*"

"Isla, your uncle died this morning, in his sleep. I need to go to Pam's right away. I'll drive you to the bus stop. I shall stay with her for a few days, but you can manage, can't you?"

"Um, yes." She had been *managing* since well before her mother had left. "Um, tell her I'm sorry," she added gauchely.

"Yes, yes," followed his hurried reply. He was on edge, his mind distracted, elsewhere.

Maybe now wasn't the time for Isla to entertain disparaging thoughts, *but why not*, she reflected. Her uncle had been nothing short of unexceptional: her aunt's echo – a cardboard cut-out, wooden. He had never shown her particular kindness, or, she supposed, unkindness, come to think of it. But anyway, the truth remained, she felt devoid of any emotion; it was as if a complete stranger to her had passed away and she really didn't care. Was this heartless? Or understandable.

"See you in a few days, then," said Peter, pulling up by the kerb. "I'll help organise the funeral and let you know when I'm back."

"OK, see you then. Bye, Father."

His impatient nod highlighted his desire to go, and door flung shut, he sped off into the distance, leaving his daughter to wait an hour for public transport, even though, like her, he had seen the school bus disappear down the road.

Indeed, Isla found the whole family situation difficult to fathom.

Her father and Pam were, without a doubt, close, in a weirdly possessive sort of way, yet were not given to outward demonstrations of affection. When her aunt's husband of seven years had appeared on the scene, Peter tolerated the man, knowing he had been chosen largely due to his inherited wealth and the fact that he was an antique restorer, which had come in extremely handy for Pam, who heavily relied on his skills to help her with everything business-related, be it restoration of furniture, paintings; even deliveries and finances were passed his way. All her needs, with no exception, were met. She was, without a shadow of a doubt, at the helm in all aspects of their relationship, and being twenty years his junior had a lot to do with this.

But latterly, and much to Pam's annoyance, the work had become too onerous for him, and he had taken to reading the paper in his favourite armchair, cup of tea by his side – but not for long! Soon, an extensive list of more sedentary tasks had been provided for the hapless man, such as emailing, accounts, purchasing etc., which could all be achieved on the computer.

Her aunt enjoyed controlling people; Peter, too, did all she required of him. Her words were adhered to without question, and if she disliked anyone, it must surely be their fault. And Pam disliked everyone.

Peter witnessed her bitterness towards Ava, which had her constantly glaring, grimacing, scowling at this attractive, slim blonde, who seemed to hold her nephew's heart, and had *wormed her way* into his house. Indeed, she did everything in her power to belittle, brandish unpleasantries, spit out sardonic remarks – she also made frequent references to Ava's job, which she referred to as a *frivolous pastime*, constantly contrasting this *lack of ambition* with her nephew's high-ranking, powerful career, forever insinuating she was not good enough. '*No offence, dear, but…*', '*Don't take this personally, but…*' she would scoff unkindly when Ava showed her a painting or announced a sale. And any attempt made to bridge the ever-widening gap had been well and truly thwarted. Yet Peter did nothing.

Then when Isla was born, Pam's jealousy increased a thousandfold. Who were these imposters, taking her nephew away from her? She, who had cared for him, loved him, provided for him, after his parents' *tragic* demise. And, while Peter, on a regular basis, observed the abrupt, discourteous, undermining jabs at his wife, he still did nothing; until, after a while, he actively blamed Ava, rather than his aunt, for any discord between them.

"*So she criticises your paintings! Well, God, you can scarcely blame her. You're hardly Monet! Or bloody Picasso, for that matter.*"

Ten minutes passed. And as the darkening clouds spat warning drops of rain, Isla's decision was instant. She would not go to school today. So, treading lightly along the already damp pavement, she commenced her walk home, pausing briefly at the corner shop to buy ice cream and cat food.

After unlocking the front door, she tossed her coat, with reckless abandon, over the banister and made a beeline for the kitchen, grabbing a spoon and plonking herself happily down on a pale wood stool to indulgently swallow the soothing cascade of honey-vanilla, which slid down her throat like an exquisite oyster.

Craving duly satiated, she secreted the remainder of her guilty pleasure, away from Father's critical eyes, in the icy depths of the freezer, prior to searching the living room for Marmalade.

And, surprised and delighted by her early return, whiskers, followed by two pointed ears and sharp, bright green eyes, shot up like a hand puppet over the top of the sofa, before the excited feline in its entirety bounced from the arm and rushed up to her, rubbing her leg and purring like a well-tuned engine.

Returning to the kitchen, cat now nestled contentedly in her arms, Isla found herself staring at the bare door frame where, once, lines used to be, neatly drawn in multi-coloured felt pens, with dates indicating each birthday from age two up until her tenth, and height measurements meticulously logged. Her father, she recalled, had been initially irritated at Ava *defacing* the paintwork, a vexation which had grown over the years, but her mother, perhaps in a bid for a small scrap of validation, had continued, gently reassuring him, when he glared disapprovingly, that the ink would wash off if they ever sold the house.

"This was my parents' home, and now it's mine. Of course I won't sell it. Why are you talking rubbish, woman?"

"I just meant the pen would do no damage to the paintwork," she said quietly.

"I thought you'd be tired of scribbling by now; you do enough of it for a living," had been his parting gibe as he left for work.

And the next morning, when they came down to breakfast, the lines had been wiped off. Isla paused, freshly inhaling Ava's slumped shoulders when she had noticed, before quickly jolting herself back to the present.

Having fed the cat and devoured a round of freshly made toast with a liberal coating of blackcurrant jam – her favourite – she made for the settee in the living room, closely followed by Marmalade. And the surrounding peace bathed her in a precious serenity, Marmalade's low purr, a soothing meditation, harmonising in perfect synchrony with her quiet breathing. It was marvellous being alone, safe in the knowledge that she would not be disturbed that day or the next. Maybe even longer.

And, effortlessly allowing her mind to drift, she closed her eyes to find herself ambling along the beach with Ava, linking hands and singing, their voices merging with birdsong and tiny waves rippling to shore.

"The whole beach is our canvas, Isla," her mother had said, "and fingers, hands, toes, our tools."

And such beautifully unique designs had been fashioned into the warm sand that day. What fun they had then, just the two of them. Alone together. And the pain of the separation intensified.

"I must see her," she blurted out loud. "On his return, I shall ask again when we might visit."

Past

Pay Heed to Wise Words

"So, how was it last night?" called Jen, breezing into the sitting room and throwing her bag onto the already cluttered tabletop. "You've got all your paints out, so I guess you feel inspired. Did you get laid?"

"Trust you to lower the tone. No, I bloody didn't! I got an innocent kiss on the lips if you must know."

"Is that all? Come on then, let's have a look at your art. Whoa… this is sex on paper – passionate colours, bubbles, balloons! Just imagine what you'd have created if you *had* got laid! There'd have been paint everywhere!" And she laughed out loud.

"You have a smutty mind, girl – pure smut."

"Nothing wrong with that. Anyhow, who's cooking tonight? Hope it's your turn."

"Actually, I've invited Peter over. He wants to see my paintings."

"Oh, I bet he does! Is that why you're adding this stirringly graphic piece to your repertoire?"

"I'm just happy, OK! It's a happy piece and if you see something else, that's fine. My work is always open to interpretation. And I'll cook. You're invited so long as you behave!"

"Oh, I can't wait. An evening of fun with pestiferous Peter."

"I don't even know what that means, but I'm pretty sure he isn't. Just be nice, OK."

"Yeah – if I must."

It was exactly 7.30pm, as arranged, when the doorbell rang. Ava had been fidgeting for over an hour, her nervous anticipation necessitating several trips to the bathroom. So, on hearing the familiar ring, she jumped, like an excitable puppy, over to the mirror to check yet again her hair and face, further ensuring her smile was radiancy epitomised as practised.

"Oh, for goodness' sake!" grouched her irritated housemate, placing her book on the arm of the settee. "Will you just calm down. Anyone would think he's the crown prince!"

"I just want to look my best is all."

"You do, honestly, and you did before you even got ready, so *go, now* and let him in."

Hurriedly adjusting her clothes once more, she took a deep breath, made for the front door and turned the handle. And there he was, huge bouquet of flowers and bottle of champagne held firmly in leather-gloved hands.

"Hi," she mouthed shyly, and gazing at the gifts, recalled the humble pasta with jarred pesto she had prepared, adding, "Oh God, I hope the meal will live up to all this!"

"Don't worry, I'm sure it will," he reassured, passing her the presents. "Um, may I come in, though? It's cold out here on the doorstep."

"Sorry! Yes, please do. The coat stand's behind you. Great you could make it." And pleasantries over, she led him into the lounge.

"You've met my friend, Jen."

"Um, yes, I believe I have." A breeze of disappointment brushed over his previously smiling face, which Jen noticed.

"Hi," she said nonchalantly. "Sit down, you're making the place look untidy."

And, somewhat put out by her bluntness, he parked himself irksomely on the nearest armchair.

Without delay, Ava opened and poured champagne, which was delivered on a plastic tray in clear juice glasses, given they had no flutes, and no wine glasses, come to that; and as he reached for his, a surprised and inadvertent: "Oh… thanks!" escaped his lips, which was again noted by Jen, prompting the words:

"I expect you're used to the real McCoy, but we don't stretch to flutes. Based on where you took Ava the other evening, I guess you're into fine dining. Maybe you could teach us some table manners, which fork to—"

"Jen, just leave it, will you," interrupted Ava. "I'm so sorry, Peter, her humour often comes across as tactlessness."

"No need to make excuses, Ava. It's OK." And he shot a stony glance at her flatmate, who, unperturbed, returned an amused grin.

"Ava says you requested to see her artwork. Is that a euphemism?"

"Jen! You promised!"

"I don't believe I appreciate your tone." And his voice verged on menacing, but swiftly collecting himself, he fell silent.

"Let's enjoy the evening, shall we? I don't know about you, but I'm starving. Come over, food's ready." And Ava rushed edgily to the kitchen to set the table.

But the damage had been done and conversation was laboured.

After the meal, Jen decided wisely to make herself scarce. Ava apologised *di nuovo* for her flatmate's comments.

"It's her warped sense of humour. She has a heart of gold once you get to know her."

"Oh, I shan't be doing that!" came the definitive response. "It's just as well she left." And his words were delivered with derisive distain. "Maybe we should see the art another time. I'm not in the mood now." And he kissed her quickly on the cheek, put on his coat and left.

"How could you!" Ava screamed the next morning. "You know I like him. You deliberately sabotaged the entire evening!"

"Oh, please, let me drink some coffee before you rip into me. I'm half asleep. You look like you've been up for hours just waiting to pounce."

And they sat in silence for a while, before Jen remarked, "I just have this distinct feeling about him; I know he's wrong for you. And it's abundantly clear he doesn't want me around. Divide and rule. Every pore in my body is telling me not to trust him, that's all."

"Well, he probably won't want to see me again after last night. I mean, who *would* after your performance? You deserve an Oscar!"

"Now, let's not get melodramatic, Ava. If he likes you, he'll ring, but my advice is, ditch him, and I say it from the bottom of my heart. If you know what's good for you, get rid, before it's too late."

"*Now* who's being melodramatic! I'm going for a drive – oh, and tonight *you're* cooking!" And, that said, she flung on her jacket, snatched up the car keys and stormed out, slamming the door behind her.

Visiting Abbie; and Peter Returns

A week later and Peter had left no messages.

"I guess that's it then. Nothing. You frightened him off good and proper."

"I did you a favour. You'll thank me one day when you meet the ideal man," replied Jen, glancing up distractedly from the paper.

"Something which, of course, does not exist – but OK, we can always fantasise."

"Yes. Oh, by the way, how long is it since you've visited your mum?"

"A couple of months. Why?"

"It's just that they're advertising cheap rail tickets to the coast. Obviously want to keep people in Britain over the summer to boost the economy. Why don't you go and see her? I'll come too if you want company."

"Can you get time off work?"

"I can easily offer staff more shifts. Several are students anyway, so they'll be glad of the extra money. So yes, in short."

"OK, good idea, let's do it. Mum'll be delighted. She likes you – God knows why!"

"Wow, that didn't take long. Thought I'd have to work harder to persuade you it's just what you need right now and beg you to invite me! But this was a piece of cake. I'll remember what a pushover you are for when I need to borrow money." And she chuckled.

Jen and family had lived in Cornwall until her father died. She and Ava had attended the local school, which was where their close friendship blossomed. But after his death, her mother had wanted a complete change of place to help her cope with his demise, so she, and her daughter, then sixteen, relocated to London where she purchased a small coffee shop.

And Jen now owned this business: Sweet Retreat, which had been left to her in her mother's will. It was ideal, as, first, she sensed her mother nearby: her endearing smile, the citrusy perfume she used to wear; and second, she already knew the business like the back of her hand, having spent many a happy hour serving local customers and tourists to London, also helping to bake the hugely popular signature croissants – and muffins to die for!

The business benefitted Ava too (who, in her late teens, had succumbed to the lure of the city, and Jen's constant pleas) in that she could display her vibrant, eye-catching art on the whitewashed walls with her name printed on a 'Local Artist' card, accompanied by an affordable price tag. Many pieces had been sold this way. Americans keen to take a little piece of England home with them, and locals, too, wishing to brighten up their living spaces.

On arrival at the Cornish coast, glorious ocean views greeted the city girls with open arms, and a noisy chorus of discordant seagulls proudly delivered an exuberant fanfare, as they circled cheerily over the fish-laden waters. And the slow pace here lulled the friends into a state of luxurious tranquility, somewhat of a rarity in the city.

As they approached her mother's drive, Ava enjoyed a tingle of exhilaration, anticipation, and she could not help but wonder why she had swapped this peaceful, picture-postcard location in favour of the dull-grey bustle of London – sheer madness!

A moment later, the taxi's horn sounded fervently, inducing a silver-haired, beaming woman, soft linen dress loosely highlighting her slender form, to fling open her front door and fly gracefully into the sun-drenched garden.

"It's so wonderful to see you both!" she called excitedly, throwing her arms round them. "Where have you been these last two months, Ava? I've hardly heard from you! Oh, I'm so glad you're here, so very glad!" she gasped, embracing her daughter a second time. "And Jen! You too… you both look radiant."

"Thanks, Abbie, you're looking good yourself. I've just brought your daughter for a visit before you forget what she looks like." And she laughed.

"Thank God you did," replied Abbie, grinning. "It's about time! I'll bring some orange juice and shortcake. Sit down on the veranda and enjoy the view."

And what a stunning view it was! Sun-soaked sea, tiny, red-feathered sailing boats like exquisite birds flapping daintily in the warm breeze. Herring gulls, with their evocative cry and Pinocchio noses, diving slickly into the liquid blue; butterflies circling the fragrant lavender, until the sun, wrapped in its warm, orange cloak, prepared to set. This was home.

"Let's go for a swim tomorrow morning," suggested Ava presently, "and afterwards, buy fish and chips coated in cider vinegar, followed by homemade fudge. What d'you say?"

"Awesome! That's what," replied Jen, licking her lips with relish. "But now, we should open some bubbly to celebrate this beautiful reunion. I'll ask your mum." And, knowing from experience a chilled bottle would already be waiting in the fridge, she made for the kitchen.

The evening embraced the sweet flavour of memories and song as they gazed in wonderment at the bright visage of the sentient moon patiently observing from the vast, star-stroked heavens.

The next day, the two friends swam in the ocean before devouring fresh cod and crispy chips; and after a brisk walk stood watching the wickedly sweet fudge being spread out lavishly on a waiting metal table. And Ava's mother joined them later in the afternoon for a cream tea by the harbour.

"I swear I must have put on an entire stone today," giggled Ava, patting her stomach.

"Ah, who cares! Have another piece of clotted cream fudge. Go on, be a devil," coaxed Jen, avidly rustling the paper bag.

And come early evening, the women cheerfully spilled into the cottage, full to the very brim with choice Cornish fare coated in calm contentment.

It was 10.30pm when the phone sounded from her bag, and surprised at the late hour, Ava rushed into the hallway, rummaging amongst tissues, purse, flyers for boat rides round the coast and a bottle-opener... *lest the need arise*, until at last, its ringtone persisting, she managed to grab the elusive mobile.

"*Ava? It's Peter. Sorry it's taken a while for me to get in touch, but work's been manic, and I had to help my aunt set up an antique vase display in the shop. I called at your apartment on several occasions, but you didn't answer. Are you OK?*"

"*Hi there. Yes fine, thanks. I wasn't expecting to hear from you after last time.*"

"*Yes, well, maybe I overreacted. I'm just not used to people like that.*"

"*It's Jen's way. She has a dry humour. Don't read anything into it. Anyway, right now, I'm in Cornwall at my mum's. We're staying here for a week.*"

There was a pause before he spoke. "*We?*"

"*Yes. Me and Jen.*"

"*Oh. Never mind... um, I mean, good. I simply wanted to ask if you'd like to go out one evening. And maybe I could see that art display this time round.*" He chuckled.

"*That'd be nice. I'll be back next week.*" Had she agreed too quickly?

"*Great. Thursday's good for me. What about 7pm at yours?*" came his rather keen suggestion.

"*Um... fine. I look forward to it.*"

"*OK, good. See you soon. Bye for now.*" And the phone went dead.

Approaching her somewhat bemused friend, having overheard enough of the dialogue to understand, Jen tutted in exasperation.

"And there it is." She sighed disapprovingly. "Pesky Peter returns to the fold and the fish simply falls into the net without so much as a struggle. What can I say? You're an idiot, but it's your life, Ava – your life."

"Yes, I know. And anyway, I'm not committing to anything, just giving someone I happen to like another chance."

"OK, whatever you say. I'm going to hit the sack now. See you tomorrow. Night."

"Night." And slipping outside to the now dark veranda, Ava stared felicitously into the star-studded sky.

Time, like a fast train, shot by, leaving in its trail a bunch of happy memories – vivid blues of the ocean, vibrant geranium-red and petunia-pink, succulent savours, soft embraces, soothing words – a treasured peace generating inner strength, completing her.

And a week on, here she was awaiting a third evening with Peter. This time donning her red mini dress – a more jazzed-up, youthful vibe, she had reasoned. And at 7pm on the dot, he had arrived. Thankfully, Jen was at a hardcore Aerobics class and was moving on to a wine bar afterwards.

"You've got to strike a balance between work and leisure," were the words of wisdom she had smugly imparted before jumping into her taxi.

Ava's date was provided with a glass of select Pinot poured into wine glasses she had purchased after last time – *just in case* – and had later been led up the stairs to a cluttered studio next to her bedroom.

"So, what do you think?" she asked, shyly indicating recently painted abstracts which had, earlier that day, been painstakingly mounted, on now-illumined easels.

"Um… wow… very interesting. Unique," he stated somewhat flatly. And there was a quiet pause before she spoke.

"You don't like them."

"Oh – on the contrary, yes… um… they're vibrant – and expressive."

And she smiled, happily absorbing this compliment, at the same time choosing to return downstairs with her guest, to avoid further elaboration.

Their dialogue flowed easily, as did the wine. Peter again mentioned his aunt and her lucrative vocation (and, judging by his tone, it was abundantly clear that Pam ruled the roost). Also touched on was life in the private school he had attended – with worrying tales of bullying, which had been totally ignored by the authorities; and which, due to their demise, he had never had the chance to mention to his parents – followed, on a lighter note, by his penchant for oysters – a seafood she had never tasted, although the very idea of swallowing something live was, in her opinion, nothing short of repugnant.

"You look nice in that dress," he remarked, suddenly edging forward.

"Thanks."

"All shiny… and sparkly."

She giggled.

And, gazing amorously into her soft, green eyes, he whispered, "Can I stay?"

"Oh, yes," came the instant reply. "Of course. I thought you'd never ask."

Just a few days later, Peter phoned to say he had purchased tickets for the cinema. The film was not to her taste, involving an overdose of shoot-outs and fast cars, and she had not the faintest idea who was who. He had insisted she would enjoy it if she gave it a chance, but she most certainly had not, thus feigning enthusiasm in the hope there was no sequel. A bar, also recommended by Peter, was their post-cinema venue and she partook of several G and Ts, while he raved about the unrivalled action shots, until they eventually returned to the flat.

"She's not in, is she?" he asked as Ava turned the key in the lock.

"Jen? No, she's gone to a concert and is staying with a friend."

"Thank God!" he mumbled.

"She's not that bad. You should give her a chance."

"I don't understand why she's your friend. You are so much better than her. The way she dresses, all that make-up – ugh, so uncouth and *loud*—"

"Let's talk about something else, shall we?" interrupted Ava, upset by his harsh criticism. "Glass of wine?"

"Have you got red?"

"Yes, it's the one you like."

"Perfect. I guess I'll stay then." And with a satisfied smirk, he stretched out comfortably on the sofa.

The Following Evening

Yanking the door shut behind her, Jen tossed her coat in the general direction of the coat stand and sighed as she made for the kitchen, poured some much-needed wine, and threw herself gratefully onto the sofa. She'd been at work since early morning, baking, preparing lunches, scrubbing tables; Saturdays were always the busiest, today being no exception.

"So good to be home!" she exclaimed. "Ava! Are you around?"

No reply.

"Ava!"

"Be right there," came a voice from upstairs. "Down in a sec."

Digging out a couple of ready meals from their icy den at the back of the fridge, Jen pierced the film and slung them in the microwave.

"Cordon bleu dining experience awaits you, ma'am," she chirped as Ava appeared in the doorway.

"Great, I'm starving. I've been painting all day. I'll show you later."

"Yes, please! Oh, and I sold another of your pictures this afternoon, just before closing time – that one with the brightly coloured boats – to an Italian woman, who manages a small gallery in Sienna. Guess how much she paid?"

"Not a clue."

"£500 – in cash! Thought it was unique – loved its dreamy impressionist mood."

"Wow! Wonderful! The money will certainly come in handy. How will she get it back to Italy? It's huge!"

"She and her husband – who was gorgeous, by the way – are touring round Europe in a camper van, so no problem at all with transit."

"Sounds romantic."

"I guess so. And talking of romance, how's pernicious Peter?"

"Will you give up! He's OK, but, I have to admit, his taste in films sucks. I was so bored yesterday, and he went *on and on* about car chases and stuff in the pub afterwards."

"Sounds like a riveting evening. But it beats me why you didn't *tell* him you were bored. *So*, anyway, are you going off him yet?"

"Sorry, no. It was good when we came back here."

"What, you mean the sex?"

"Yeah, that too. We talked… oh and he wants me to meet his aunt. Not sure about that, but I said yes."

"God, Ava. Why on earth would you want to meet *her*? This shitshow gets more thrilling by the minute." And she gave an exaggerated yawn. "How long have we had these ready meals? Mine tastes like gorgonzola, but it said 'tuna' on the sleeve."

Ava grinned as she plonked herself down by her friend. "I do love you, you crazy woman."

Present

Uncle Clive's Funeral

Saturday dawned. The shiny, black car, crawling with hearse-like respect, neared the grey forecourt, and Isla and her father, met by a veil of drizzle newly puncturing the steely grey skies, slowly alighted, shutting the door quietly behind them.

In the damp church yard, a sea of strangers hovered, speaking in low, barely audible tones – the tones of death; and an eclectic array of dark dresses, suits, ties, ebony gloves, black-lace hats and feather fascinators accompanied their quiet, mournful looks and melancholy faces.

Aunt Pam's lugubrious expression, set like jelly, had successfully replaced that of scorn and derision; yet no tears were shed, the only visible indication of movement being the vein pulsing on her scrawny neck, as she mechanically greeted folk she'd probably never met.

Was she upset? Isla wondered. Or so used to concealing more gentle feelings, deemed as weakness, that they had disappeared altogether, if indeed they had ever existed. Then again, maybe she would crumble and collapse, distraught, in the privacy of her home, wretchedly embracing one of her more valuable antique vases? Or *maybe…* she wouldn't put it past her aunt to have bumped Clive off. *Stop it, Isla*, she chided herself. *This is neither the time, nor the place!* But the tiniest of smiles flickered for a split second across her otherwise sombre face, causing her to focus with intense concentration on the dismal service, to ensure it would not return.

Woefully solemn hymns commanded the nave. Speeches with sorrowful, shaking voices issued from the lectern: *he was a good man, kind, thoughtful…* traits she had personally not experienced; it was as if they were talking about someone else, as if she were at the wrong funeral. Cucumber and salmon sandwiches, egg and cress too, were nibbled half-heartedly, with careful attention paid to prevent any cress wedging itself between unwary teeth. And scarily fragile china cups perched on wafer-thin saucers were balanced precariously in tensed hands, with small sips of tea being steadily ingested from time to time amid doleful sighs. Delicate eclairs and a selection of cheese, crackers and grapes were also on offer to the desolate throngs, in a desperate ploy to delay their leaving this dreary venue too soon.

And, after the last few mourners had trailed off, that was it. Over.

Ashes to ashes. Dust to dust.

Amen.

Monday. As they drove to school, the sun skilfully scaled the candyfloss clouds, and on reaching the fluffy summit, confidently peeked out onto a new day.

"Father," ventured Isla, filling the silence. "We need to choose where we want to go for work experience. I was thinking of the new art gallery in town. They have placements there – I asked my teacher. And it's only a short bus journey. I'd really love to go."

There was a slight pause, where she waited in nervous anticipation.

"That will not be possible, Isla," he replied, immediately crushing her hopes. "You'll be working with Pam for the week. Now that Uncle's died, she'll be more than glad of the extra support."

"But Father—"

"I won't hear another word about it, Isla. It will be highly beneficial for you to see exactly how the business is run. Much more appropriate than a week in an *art gallery*, that's for sure."

So, as usual there was no more to be said. And a nagging knot like a closed fist settled inside her.

Peaks and Valleys

Final exams would take place at the end of the academic year, rendering this the last of the parents' evenings. Letters had been posted to all just in case some pupils *forgot* to deliver by hand, which had proved a significant problem in the past.

These evenings, however, were embraced by Isla, whose refuge from inner turmoil was indubitably her school, classmates, and study, which provided a calm and much-needed distraction, helping no end with her confidence and wellbeing.

Her father had booked a late slot to fit in with his tight work schedule and had rushed home direct from the office so they could leave immediately for the school. And she had dressed in mufti attire: muted-pink jumper and black skirt, for the occasion.

Sitting on one of the two wooden chairs placed in front of each teacher and wishing her mother could have been there, Isla, nevertheless, basked in the moment, while staff sang her praises to her waiting father.

"Your daughter is a model student," her tutor had

declared. "We are delighted with her exemplary mock exam results and have no doubt she will do herself justice in the public exams later this year."

After this came the careers teacher, who sat expectantly on the other side of an old, oak desk, which had been freshly polished for the occasion.

"Are you going to the art gallery for your work experience, Isla, as we discussed?" she asked.

Isla stared into her lap.

"Um—" she started but was instantly interrupted by her father, who spoke in loud, decisive tones.

"Unfortunately, Isla's uncle died very recently, prompting a change of plan. So my daughter will be spending her work experience at her aunt's antique shop, where her help will be much needed at this difficult time."

"Oh dear, I am sorry for your loss. Yes, of course. I'm sure that will be fine. I'll update the placement."

Attempting to hide her disappointment, Isla smiled weakly as they rose to leave.

Finally, her English teacher, again delighted, waxed lyrical over her amazing insight, powerful contribution to discussion and exemplary written assessments.

On the journey home, a slight remorse for sabotaging his daughter's choice of placement rose in Peter's throat, rapidly to be devoured. This could, however, have contributed to him voicing those rare words: "Well done, Isla, well done," words which induced a pleasant ripple to rush through her. And she repeated this compliment to herself over and over like a new and treasured maxim: "Well done, Isla, well done!"

It was now six weeks since Ava had gone, and Isla had decided that this would be the day to pluck up courage to ask again if they might visit. Father was at home due to a bank holiday, so now seemed like the perfect time, or at least, this is what she told herself while avidly rehearsing the words she would use to express this urgent request. She knew already that he would say no, so what then? She would have to persist, stand resolute. It was her right; he could not keep her away forever.

So, once they had eaten dinner, and expertly hiding her mounting agitation, she finally found her voice and broached the subject.

"Father, we haven't visited mother since she left, please could we go this weekend? I'm sure she would be delighted to see us, and I miss her so much."

"Not this again, Isla. I've explained, she probably won't even know us or care if we're there or not. It's all for the best to keep our distance and let the doctors look after her."

"But I wish to go and see for myself. If you don't want to, you could take me and leave me at the entrance; I could visit alone and meet you in the car park later. Please, Father."

"For Christ's sake, Isla! You're just like her! Why can't you take no for an answer?"

"Because this is important. I wish to see my mother. It's been six whole weeks!"

"No, Isla. No. It's not happening."

"Then I'll talk to my teacher, ask her advice." Where had she discovered this warrior-like defiance in her tone?

"You'll do no such thing!"

"Well, take me then."

"Don't you dare blackmail me, child. Go to your room! Now!"

"Yes, Father."

And, with calm reserve, Isla left, realising she had probably said enough for the moment; but she remained proud of herself, wondering where all this, thus far, hidden resolve had hailed from. Somehow, the more she had spoken, the more easily her words flowed; she had, albeit belatedly, finally managed to tap into her formally tethered tenacity, had now given him food for thought, time to reflect; and if he remained adamant, she would indeed involve the school authorities.

Sadly, her fleeting heroism had disappeared in a cloud of dust come morning, and dread seized the child as she prepared to face her hitherto fuming father.

Her entry to the kitchen was soundless, yet her father, who was leaning against the table, spun round instantly.

"Good morning," she mumbled, struggling to form the required words.

He reciprocated with a brief nod.

"Isla," he said. "I have been thinking about your desire to see your mother."

The child froze.

"And have decided you shall visit next weekend."

The room fell silent – until a steady realisation, like the gradual emergence of unexpected sunlight, dusted her pale face with a faint pink flush, which swiftly grew to a grateful smile, prompting her to look her father in the eye. But was the wall between them too solid for her to tread through or climb up? Gingerly, she neared, her thin arms lightly reaching out and around his scratchy wool jacket.

"Thank you," she muttered as she stepped hastily back to safety.

Her pleasure, however, was transient.

"On Friday evening, we shall drive to Aunt Pam's and stay until Saturday. I phoned her yesterday to inform her of your mother's whereabouts. Of course, she was shocked. Who wouldn't be! But at least the secret is out now. On Saturday afternoon, she will accompany you to the psychiatric unit, where you'll spend some time with Ava. I'll wait for you both outside."

"But please – can't I go in alone?" The very thought of her reproving aunt's gloating manner made her sick to the core.

"Are you never satisfied? Maybe the whole idea was a mistake; we could always cancel!"

"No, no, it's fine. Thank you. I'll fetch my school bag."

And she hastened to her room, where she threw herself on the bed, burying her face in the covers.

Her aunt's house harboured a multitude of treasured antiques, some of which were, in fact, priceless (according to Aunt Pam anyway), and Isla crept cautiously through the entrance hall, past porcelain vases and marble statuettes on soundly structured plinths, worried-to-death she might knock them over despite their robustly solid location. *And what would happen if she did?* What if, in a frenzy of revenge for all the disparaging insults, insinuations, accusations she had suffered over the years, she could finally release all her pent-up rage and simply destroy everything precious to her aunt, shatter every desirous artifact, every adored possession, in a riotous, rebellious revolt?

But, alas, her father's clamorous call was to cut viciously through her vivid musings.

"Isla! What's the matter with you? For God's sake, don't just stand there, come through and greet Pam."

And, as expected, her aunt lost no time in pouncing on her captive prey.

"So, dear, I hear we're going to visit your mother in the mental asylum tomorrow! Well, I certainly never expected that. I'm not at all surprised though. We should have seen it coming."

And, with nowhere to hide, Isla's crimson face, like the fragile vases, was now on full display for all to see, her recent dream of insurrection having turned to ashen dust.

Past

Weekend Away

"Let's go and visit your mother for a few days," said Peter out of the blue. "I'd like to meet her. You take that woman, Jen, often enough."

"Not this again! *That woman?* Come on, Peter, be nice."

"OK, but let's go. It'd be fun."

"Yes, why not. We'll drive down at the weekend. I'll phone Mum this afternoon."

And thus, it was settled. A trip to the sea!

Shame Peter didn't like swimming – *water's too salty, too cold!* Or sitting on the sand – *gets everywhere!*

Never mind.

On arrival, Peter presented Abbie with an elaborate bouquet of roses, and his smile had been radiancy itself. They had exchanged pleasantries over Earl Grey and shortbread before Ava suggested they drive to a pebbly cove to partake in some fishing.

"Sounds good," enthused Peter, politely bidding Abbie goodbye.

"We'll bring some fish back for supper, Mum. See you later." And she blew her mother a kiss.

The secluded bay was all-but empty, thus rendering a large selection of vessels available. And once a little blue rowing boat had been selected, they were soon riding on the gently foaming waves. Ava inhaled a buzz of exhilaration as she felt certain Peter would enjoy the day.

Sure enough: "I think I've caught something," he gasped after just half-an-hour. "It's *huge* and straining at the rod! I've struck the jackpot, Ava! Oh, my God, I can't hold it!" he shouted wildly. "Help Ava, help!"

So, heaving and hauling in unison, they eventually dragged, not a prize catch, nor a treasure chest, but a colossal clump of stony seaweed to the boat's edge, which made her giggle.

"Don't!" he snapped, a rising anger colouring his cheeks. "It's not bloody fair." And he sulked, childlike in his disappointment, and vexed at her reaction. "I actually thought I had something. I can't be bothered with this any longer. Let's go back to shore."

"Don't be defeatist. You need to persevere with these things. And we promised Mum we'd bring some fish home for tea."

"I am *not* defeatist! We'll just buy some fresh from the market and pretend we caught it. OK?"

"Shame on you, Peter Mills!" replied Ava, but noting distinct irritation in his eyes, she reluctantly concurred. "OK, I guess we could do that. Do you want to go back now then?"

"Yes, but first we'll pop into the pub, and then purchase some cod, before heading back to your mum's. I'll drive."

En route they approached a wooden, almost cartoon-like, bridge arching over a narrow, rippling stream, and Ava called out, "Oh wait! Let's stop here!"

"Why?" he asked, pulling over.

"Me and Jen used to play here as kids – Pooh Sticks. You throw a stick in on one side of the bridge and wait for it to emerge at the other side. The one whose stick arrives first is the winner. We used to love it. Let's have a go, just for fun," she said opening her door and stepping onto the grassy verge.

"For God's sake, Ava. How old are you – six? I can well believe that idiot friend of yours liked it. Come on, get in; let's be on our way."

And humiliated, she inched herself onto the passenger seat.

Why had she let this pass? Why hadn't she said anything?

Never mind.

Initially, Abbie had been impressed by Peter's charm, but as the weekend progressed, she observed her daughter slightly less forthright than usual, with Peter often cutting in as she spoke, and this caused her concern.

"Do you like him, Mum?" probed Ava, following her mother into the garden.

"Yes, of course; he's charming. But just make sure to stay your lovely, spirited self, won't you?" she mentioned diplomatically.

"What do you mean?"

"Well, he's a little domineering at times."

"I hadn't noticed," she replied, quietly reflecting on their day.

Shortly after their return home, Ava was taken ill.

"Must be food poisoning," she deduced. "Shellfish – in that local restaurant. It only takes one."

"Could be. But what about tonight?" griped Peter. "We were supposed to go to Pam's. She'll have prepared dinner and will not be best pleased if we don't turn up."

Ava didn't care. She had already endured a brief audience with Pam, when Peter had wanted to pop into the shop to introduce her, and had found the woman standoffish, aloof, and clearly resentful of her relationship with Peter.

"Well, can't be helped," came her irritated reply, fuelled further by the memory of this unpleasant woman. "I need to be in bed. And a bit of sympathy wouldn't go amiss."

"What good's that going to do? Look, I think I'll go. At least then the food won't be wasted. Don't want to upset Pam."

"Oh, perish the thought!" she said sarcastically amid retching into the toilet basin.

"You could at least be a bit quieter," he teased, adding, "anyhow, I'll pop round tomorrow. See you later." And he strode downstairs, slamming the front door behind him.

"Charming!" she snarled, throwing herself onto the bed and pulling the quilt over her head.

Throughout the ensuing day, the dreadful nausea continued to possess poor Ava's body with an unrelenting vigour, causing her to vomit with such frequency as to leave her exhausted. It wasn't until late afternoon that she ventured downstairs for water.

"You look awful," said Jen, plonking her shopping bags on the tabletop. "Why aren't you in bed?"

"I have been, like all day! I feel *so* sick. I ate some dodgy seafood. Never again!"

"Yes, could well be that… *or*…"

"Or what?"

"Well… maybe you're pregnant."

"Pregnant? Don't be daft."

"Come on, you must have considered it. Makes perfect sense."

"I've been careful. It's impossible."

"Yeah, but still, I think you'll find it's not. Listen, wait here and I'll buy you a pregnancy kit. I need to reassure myself there will be no mini-me Peters popping up any time soon."

"Very funny, but thanks, Jen."

A short while later, Ava emerged from the bathroom, her face a picture of incredulity.

"I was right," exclaimed Jen. "I knew it. So what are you intending to do?"

"Um… I have absolutely *no* clue whatsoever! How could this possibly have happened? I just don't get it."

"Well, I could explain the facts of life, but given your current situation, I'm pretty sure you already know," she teased. "Oh, and *please* tell me that pest of a Peter is not going to feature in our future lives – I mean yours."

"I need to go and see him, tell him – like right away," declared Ava.

"Sit down. I'll get some wine – for me, and a cup of tea for you. There's no hurry. He can wait. OK? Give yourself time to process this news before you make any hasty decisions."

"OK," muttered Ava, resignedly lowering herself onto the sofa.

Revelations

How could this have happened? The words whirled relentlessly round her head like a spinning-top, soon, however, to be superseded by: *How shall I tell Peter?*

"I'll come straight out with it, that's the best way."

Had she really said these words out loud? She sighed as, amidst curious glances, the tube slid snake-like to the next platform. *Her* platform. From here it was just a five minute walk to a small Greek taverna where she had arranged to meet Peter. She had felt it best for the rendezvous to take place somewhere public. Why, she wasn't entirely sure; it simply felt right this way. What kind of reaction was she expecting? Did she have any inkling? Was she secretly anticipating a favourable one? Or… who knew? Anyhow, she was here now, there was no turning back. And she took a deep breath, as she ruffled her hair and smoothed down her dress, before entering the cosy, dimly lit room, a room which, considering the diminutive space, housed surprisingly large pictures brightly adorning fresh, whitewashed walls; images of Greek sunsets and bougainvillea-stroked, blue-roofed buildings against a backdrop of idyllic, azure skies.

And there he was, glass of red wine in hand, settled at a small table for two in a snug little alcove set back slightly from the window.

Throwing a brief smile in his direction, and careful not to appear too nervous, she stepped over to the wooden table, gently lowering herself onto the cushioned chair.

"Hi, what took you so long?"

"I'm on time. You must have got here early," she replied, eager to get this news over with.

"Maybe." He shrugged. "Well, it's nice to see you. I'll order some more wine."

"Oh, no thanks. Just an orange juice for me."

"Orange juice? Are you ill?"

"No," she muttered, "I'm fine… but…"

"But what?"

And unable to contain herself, she blurted out, "I'm pregnant."

There was silence. Peter stared into space, stupefied, until after a long and awkward pause, he spoke.

"But…"

"Yes, I know. I don't understand it either."

A stern, defensive glint formed in his eyes.

"Have you slept with anyone else?"

"Of course not!" came her defiant response. "How can you even think that?"

"Well, what are you planning to do?" A muted hostility crept through his words.

"I don't know." Her voice was now a mere whisper. Why had she dared hope he'd be happy?

"I need to think, to process this – on my own," he

stated matter-of-factly. "I'll get the bill." And he signalled to the waiter.

"You're leaving already? But I only just arrived."

"Yes, but you've just dropped a massive bombshell! Is it so hard to understand that right now I need to be alone? You've had time to digest all this, I haven't."

"OK, that's fine. Take all the time you need. I'll go home and have lunch with Jen." His cold reaction had left her stunned, and tears, which she struggled to quash, welled in her eyes.

"Well, for God's sake, don't tell *her*," he hissed.

"She knows already. And why on earth does it matter?" A weak flush rippled through her body, and she thought she might faint.

"You told *her* before *me!*" He breathed in exaggeratedly, in an attempt to control his rising resentment, before adding, "That's bloody typical!"

"How can you hate her so much?" cried Ava in a momentary burst of indignation, which almost instantly she regretted. Why had she raised her voice? Everyone seemed to be staring at her and a deep red flush appeared on her distraught face.

"I'm going," she muttered, hurriedly rising from her seat, and the poor girl hastened out of the restaurant, ashamedly sensing a sea of nosy diners scrutinising her every move until she stepped thankfully out into the daylight.

However, as she traipsed mechanically along the street towards the metro, from a distance she heard her name being called over and over.

"Ava, Ava, stop, please stop. Ava!"

Her senses were suddenly alerted, and she turned to see Peter running to catch up with her.

"Ava, please wait. I'm sorry, OK. I didn't have a chance – to think; but I suddenly realised, as soon as you'd left, I know already. I love you. I want to have a child with you. I do, Ava. Move in with me, move in with me now. I'll look after you. I'll be there for you, I promise. I love you, Ava."

"Do you though?" she said, still angry, yet quietly overjoyed he'd followed her.

"Of course I do, darling. I won't ever let you down."

His eyes were so beautiful, so sincere, so remorseful. And she relented. Completely. Fell into his arms.

"So, will you let me be a part of your life, Ava? Will you move in with me?" And he waited anxiously for her response.

"Yes," she exclaimed, holding him close. "Yes, I will!"

Future Plans Disclosed

After having spoken to Peter, Ava's frayed nerves, along with her churned-up stomach, had settled, and she had managed to blot out the earlier episode in the restaurant. After all, he'd come good in the end.

They had stopped off at a pleasant café near the metro and had talked for the best part of the afternoon, which had certainly been beneficial, leaving her future direction much clearer. Settling down with Peter was, she realised, what she had wanted all along.

As she strolled through the busy streets, however, she could not help but worry about Jen. Moving out of the flat they had shared for many years would naturally be a wrench, and she doubted very much that Jen would relish living there on her own, unless, of course, she advertised for another flatmate. So on nearing the apartment, she drew in a deep breath to brace herself for their ensuing dialogue.

"Jen, I have something I need to tell you," she said, after pouring a glass of water and perching on the settee beside her friend.

"Brilliant! Spill the beans then. Let me guess, you

saw sense, the irascible runt is finally out of your life, you told him to sling his hook. Did he run a mile when you informed him about the pregnancy? You did tell him, didn't you?"

"Yes."

"Well, how did he react?"

Ava decided to omit the initial chapter and focus solely on the latter part of their day. "Um, he seemed happy enough," she ventured.

"So what now? What is your pressing news?"

"Um, look, the truth is…" She paused, before adding, "He's actually asked me to move in with him." And she managed a weak smile while awaiting the response.

"You've got to be kidding me, Ava! You can't be serious," cried Jen incredulously. "He's bad news. You need to tread carefully and moving in with him is falling straight into his trap."

"Listen, will you! I've made my decision and you've been my friend long enough to know that I am fully capable of standing up for myself."

"Around him, I'm not so sure."

"He wants to arrange a meal out so that you two can try to be on good terms. I told him you are important to me, and he agreed to give things another go. You will come, won't you? It means a lot to me that you both get on."

Silence flushed through the room before Jen responded.

"OK," she said sullenly. "But I'm only doing this for you – not your anal-retentive beau."

"Thank you, *I think*." She grinned. "It means a lot."

Dining with the Enemy

An *haute cuisine* restaurant had been selected by Peter. When Ava had questioned his choice, he insisted, saying: "Nothing but the best for you and your friend. I merely wish to make a good impression." Did she discern sarcasm?

She had wanted to scream that Jen would not be remotely enamoured by such a gesture, that she would far prefer, *dare she say it*, a less pretentious, more relaxed venue – and she was right.

"Oh, what? You're joking. One nil to provocative Peter! But no matter," said Jen, smirking. "I shall show my appreciation by my dress choice."

"Jen, please don't stir things. This is supposed to be another chance for you both to make peace with each other."

"OK, fine," she relented, noting Ava's angst. "Again, just for you, I'll dress appropriately."

"Great. So, all settled then. We'll meet him in the West End on Friday night at 7pm."

"Noted. I'm inscribing this momentous occasion on my calendar as we speak." And she winked.

Cream-tiled walls, mosaic flooring and a huge window framed in thin, black wood, adorned with a gold letter M in the centre, greeted the pair as they strolled arm in arm, Ava in a mushroom, cowl-necked silk top and black skirt, Jen in black leather trousers and a green linen jumper.

"So this is how the other half live," she joked. "I look forward to embracing the experience."

"Peter said to meet up in the foyer and, once we've all arrived, the waiter will escort us to our table."

"Speak of the devil," said Jen, looking behind her. "And who on earth is that woman?"

"Oh no!" declared Ava. "That's his aunt. Why in heaven's name did he bring her?"

"Well, we can't do anything about it now; they're nearly here. *What is she wearing?* God, that necklace is *big*! Are those stones diamonds? And that handbag, *so shiny*! Faux fur shoulder cape – very tasteful! It is faux fur, isn't it?"

"Probably not, knowing her." Ava sighed.

"Come on then, let's go and greet Cruella and her sidekick, Peter Pain-in-the-Proverbial."

Ava could hardly suppress a giggle. Having Jen here made her so much more relaxed.

"Pam. Pleased to meet you," stated his aunt, extending a gloved hand as she approached. And the vein on her neck twitched.

"Jen, likewise." The lie came easily.

"And Ava. We meet again. How nice." And her cold gaze made Ava shudder.

Peter smiled, first at Ava, then rigidly at Jen, who reciprocated with a civil nod.

"This way, madam," gushed the waiter, his enthusiasm as fake as Pam's pleasantries, as he led the way to a formally decorated corner table, where he helped them to be seated, after relieving Peter of his paisley-lined, slate-grey jacket and Pam of her dead animal cape.

Shortly he returned, fashioning a creepy Uriah Heep bow whilst distributing large sepia menus, tucked in at the corners to brown leather holders.

"Drinks, madam?" he said, covetously ogling Pam's necklace.

"Two bottles of Champagne for the table," she replied curtly, pointing to her required vintage.

"Um, I'd prefer a glass of Pinot Grigio," said Jen. "Ava?"

"Coke, please." She sensed Peter staring disapprovingly at her friend and averted her eyes.

Also noting his annoyance, Jen continued, "Actually, could you bring me a *bottle* of Pinot," while deliberately directing a sassy smirk at Peter, who reciprocated with an icy glare. *How dare she diverge from his aunt's especially chosen champagne?* And seething impotently, he clenched his fist under the table.

"*Pour hors d'oeuvre: escargots*, puff pastry; *et plat principal: roti avec legumes*," emphasised Pam, on the waiter's return, proudly demonstrating her best French accent; however, pronouncing the words *pâte feuilletée* had clearly proved a tad too arduous for her English tongue, *puff pastry* being more palatable, plosive, pertinent.

"Wow, that's good," piped Jen insincerely, before adding, "I should capture some snails from the garden

– they're beggars for eating geranium leaves but bung them in a pan with garlic butter and basil and, *hey presto*, you've got your very own gourmet dish – and local at that!"

Ava struggled not to laugh. Pam and Peter struggled not to unleash their ire at what, to them, constituted brazenness.

Amusedly glimpsing their irritation, and ignoring the waiter vying for her attention, Jen eventually deemed it apt to speak.

"Um... onion soup – *soupe à l'oignon*, and fish and chips – that is to say, *poisson et pommes frites*."

"And what would madam desire?" asked the little man, his feigned interest transparent, as he turned to Ava.

"Omelette, followed by a main course of salmon, please," she said quietly.

"Soup and venison for me." Peter paused after his order and turned to his aunt, exclaiming, "Did you know, Pam, Jen is a waitress in a very small café in Camden?"

"How quaint," came the disparaging response. "So you cook, take orders, clean tables and wash up," she spouted loftily.

"Well, I actually employ staff to help me. I'm the owner, you see. The café is extremely well thought of in the area, and people love to see Ava's art displayed on the walls, too. A lot of pieces have been sold to art dealers."

"But not discerning ones," tittered Pam derisively.

There followed a lengthy pause, before Jen,

attempting to contain her wrath, replied, "And what do you do, Pam?"

"I own an antique shop in the salubrious area of Knightsbridge."

"Very nice. When I was a child, we lived above an antique shop; well, actually, quite a lot of the pieces were more like junk, but the word *antique* covers a multitude of sins, I guess." Luckily, her poker face did not betray her, though she dared not look at Ava, just in case.

"How is your venison, Peter?" snapped Pam, hell-bent on changing the subject, and the vein in her neck, mirroring her outrage, pulsed violently.

Acknowledging her displeasure and responding to her wish to move on, he replied, "Not as delicious as yours, Aunt, but fine."

And, hanging on to this compliment, she seemed somewhat appeased, outwardly at least.

Desserts were eaten in virtual silence, punctuated by awkward small talk regarding the texture of the salted caramel sorbet and the merits of honeycomb flakes in the sticky toffee ice cream; the weather was also touched on and the popularity of the latest show in the West End. And after the dainty selection of French cheeses, with ale, buttermilk and charcoal crackers, had been consumed, Peter beckoned the waiter for the bill.

"Thank you," said Jen. "That was lovely."

"Yes," agreed Ava, although she knew, as did everyone, that a speedy exit would be a welcome release from this purgatory.

"A pleasure," mouthed Peter brusquely. "Our taxi's outside, do you want a lift to your apartment?"

"No, thanks, we've got a bit of shopping to do first. Thanks anyway." And Ava kissed Peter on the cheek before nodding farewell to his aunt. "See you soon."

"Sure," he replied quickly, as they strode out to meet their driver, leaving the two women to heave a much-needed sigh of relief.

"Wine bar?" suggested Jen.

"Oh, yes please!" beamed Ava. And they stepped outside to the freedom of the city.

"He's not usually that grouchy, you know."

"Thank the Lord, although I do beg to differ, but will refrain from telling you that you are making a huge mistake allowing pitiful Peter into your life." She smirked. "Are we at least agreed that his aunt's vile?"

"Oh yes, most definitely," chuckled Ava.

"You never mentioned you'd met her."

"Well, it was only fleeting; and you already hate Peter, so I guess I didn't want to introduce any more negative vibes into the mix." And a faint smile formed on her lips. "Come on, let's go," she said, slipping her arm through Jen's.

And they slid through the revolving door of their favourite wine bar, soon to sink into the comfy leather chairs and take in the warm orange lighting and soft music.

"I was thinking," said Ava, after several glasses of non-alcoholic wine. "Why don't we go to Cornwall? I want to tell Mum about my pregnancy, and I'd love you to come with me. What do you say?"

"I say, hell yes, that'd be great."

"Brilliant! What about next week? Saturday?"

"Perfect. You've got yourself a date. Cheers to us," and she raised her glass.

"Yes, cheers to us," agreed Ava happily.

The Rabid Rat

Having just visited the doctor for a routine check-up, Ava now ambled through the nearby park, vaguely glancing at local children roaring with excited laughter, punching the air around them in exuberant glee. Such trouble-free innocence caused a faint flicker to instinctively visit her lips as she strolled past. And continuing down the tree-lined boulevard to the edge of the park, she crossed the road and bore right to reach the chemist's, the specific vitamin requirements listed on the surgery's headed notepaper gripped protectively in her closed hand. *What a responsibility having a child must surely be! And Peter... oh God, would he measure up?*

She reflected uneasily on the continual tension between Jen and him, which, despite her attempts at reconciliation, had quietly festered over dinner; and later, something she felt sure must be heavily linked, was his violent reaction when she had announced their imminent trip to Cornwall. Why had his angry outburst startled her when this had not, by any means, been the first time? *People can change, though, can't they?* she mused hopefully.

"*Jen*?!" he had growled. "Why is *she* going with you? Couldn't you have waited till *I* was free? You were aware I had a conference this weekend. Did you organise for *this* weekend, knowing I wouldn't be around? *Bloody typical*."

"Would you kindly calm down!" she had replied, irritably shaking her head. "We organised the trip spontaneously, but *yes*, I knew you'd be away and so it made perfect sense for us to go *then*. Stop being a child."

"*A child*! OK, fine, go with *her*, and don't worry, I need to pack and then I'll be out of your hair, so you can press on with your cliquish plans." And he stomped off, like said sulky child after a reprimand, a dramatic slam of the door following his exit.

Why did he always storm off? It was as if he were incapable of discussing anything. If she disagreed with his point of view, he'd become angry and the anger would escalate until she backed down, and this reflex reaction was fast becoming a pattern, an unwholesome norm. But she should be positive. Everyone had their faults, and he could often be kind and thoughtful too. At present, her hormones were all over the place, which wasn't ideal, yet time with Jen was a tonic, leaving her relaxed, light-headed, unlike his rigid presence, where her humorously intended jesting was reacted to with decided tetchiness. Indeed, the trouble was he took himself far too seriously.

One of Jen's wealth of references for him was *the rabid rat*, which, she had to admit, was amusing, yet had this gibe drifted anywhere within earshot, Peter's wrath would have surely escalated to the fury of a raging bull.

Funny, these days, with her constant agitation and indecision, *nothing* seemed straightforward, but what *was* a certainty was the trip to Cornwall, and wild horses would not drag her away from this course! Peter would just have to grow up!

Brief Respite

They decided to drive this time, and thankfully the motorway had but a few cars, dotted like lone leopards, speeding to their respective destinations, allowing the journey to last a mere four and a half hours. Ava's excitement at the prospect of seeing her mother again rendered her highly chatty and Jen was delighted that her friend was so cheerful.

"OK, so let's plan our week," declared Ava eagerly. "You first."

"Um, well, of course we'll spend time with Abbie today, then tomorrow, chill on the beach, visit some local haunts, eat loads of fish and drink white wine – well, that's me, anyway!" She paused to draw breath. "What about you?"

Ava reflected before smiling enthusiastically.

"So… I'd like to hire a rowing boat for the day and catch some fish for our evening meal; we could maybe have a barbecue – Mum would love that," she said, certain they'd have much more fun than her short-lived trip with Peter. "And the next day we could enjoy a picnic by the river – and play Pooh Sticks," she continued, recalling his unkind words, "like we used to!" And there was a strong defiance in her tone.

"Sounds perfect, Ava," cried Jen contentedly. "Let's do it *all*!" And a blissful grin skipped onto her lips.

Once they pulled off the main road, slender, meandering country lanes, like finely curled hair, brushed alongside cushions of yellow rapeseed fields and meadowland. And before long, seagulls sailed skyward, suspended, like puppets, by a playful breeze, a constant reminder that the open sea was within reach.

"Each time I come home, I never cease to wonder why I ever left," reflected Ava. "This place is the epitome of perfection – honestly."

"We had a real blast here as kids, so many adventures, such freedom to roam. It's not the same when you're an adult, there are too many bills to pay, decisions to make, responsibilities…"

"Like having a baby, you mean?" Ava chewed her lower lip.

"Yeah, I guess so, but hey, we're not going down that road right now. Think about the present; we should allow sweet Serenity to take us into her safe, gentle arms, rock us, stroke our hair."

Ava laughed. "Yes, and we'll swim in the cool, crystal-clear seas, followed by real ale – *for you*, orange for me – in the local pub, not forgetting, of course, a packet of salt and vinegar crisps. What do you reckon?"

"I reckon that's a brilliant idea!"

Abbie's garden, flecked with flora, spread like colourful cloth to the edge of the lane and, hearing a much-awaited engine noise jet over the calm, she rushed excitedly towards the sound.

Almost toppling out of the car door, Ava threw herself into her mother's arms, and all the pent-up pressure of the last few weeks evaporated in the instant.

"Darling! So lovely to see you. And Jen! How are you both?" Her mother stood still, taking in her daughter.

"You look stressed, Ava."

"Always known for your honesty, Mum," she chuckled. "You're spot on though, as always, but don't worry, all good, and it's a long story, which I'll tell you later."

"I look forward to it. Now, I bet you're hungry after your long journey. I've made fresh pasties," she declared.

"Lovely!" they both cried in unison, and the cases were tugged like reluctant dogs out of the sun and into the hallway, before the tired yet excitable women made for the dining room.

"That was divine," praised Ava, two pasties later, licking her lips.

"Good," replied Abbie, visibly delighted. "It's a shame you didn't want wine though, that's unlike you."

Was this comment in any way pointed? Ava wasn't entirely sure. But Jen clearly thought it might be and so, with a knowing glance, urged her to divulge all, so she would be less edgy.

"OK, Mum, there's no easy way of saying this, but, um… I'm pregnant – and I'm moving in with Peter. It's all been a bit sudden; I haven't had time to process everything fully, but I was keen to see you as soon as possible in order to share my news." And she waited expectantly.

"Oh darling," said her mother with quiet composure, which expertly masked her fears. "I'm so glad you told me, and if you are certain about all of this, then I am too. Your happiness is my main priority." And this imparted, she rose quickly from her chair to administer an ebullient embrace, the relief of which caused Ava to dissolve into a flood of tears.

The three chatted until the sun went down and then, remaining in the patio garden, lit candles, watched the stars and gazed up at the moon. And, exhausted after the long journey, Ava retired early.

"See you in the morning, darling," her mother smiled, kissing her on the cheek.

"Night, Mum, see you tomorrow. Night, Jen." And she hugged her friend and disappeared up the stairs.

"She doesn't seem her usual energetic self," voiced Abbie sotto voce. "Is everything OK?"

"Well, basically, Peter made a huge, unnecessary fuss about Ava coming to Cornwall with me – he dislikes me with a vengeance, you see – aren't I the lucky one! He had a conference and couldn't come anyway, but he seems to categorically disapprove of our friendship. I have to say, I'm really not sure about him, but, at the end of the day, it's Ava's decision, isn't it? Also, I think the pregnancy was a bit of a shock, but she appears to be getting her head round it now; just needs time."

"I did hazard a guess regarding that, to be truthful. I must say though, I'm not so sure about Peter either. When he came to visit, aside from his initial charm, I found him a little domineering. He persisted in correcting Ava and finishing her sentences. I didn't like that. She's so confident normally, but she was decidedly quieter with him around."

"Yes, I know. I've advised her on several occasions to take things slowly and to be careful, but now she's pregnant, events have started to speed up considerably."

"I think we should talk to her."

"She won't listen, I've already tried, but OK, we'll give it one last shot."

The next day saw the two friends on the rickety bridge, hurling their respective sticks into the brook. It was a trip down memory lane to their all but idyllic childhoods.

"I won! Yours was too slow – *sooo* slow!" And Jen roared with laughter.

"*No*, it was not! Yours pushed mine out of the way and it got stuck in the rushes until that duck nudged it out, but yours had already won by then!"

"Yeah, well, that's life I guess; there are winners and…" She fashioned an 'L' sign with her fingers.

Ava's gasp of mock indignation soon transformed into a broad grin as she skipped over the bridge, and took off her shoes, dipping her warm feet into the icy-cold water, just like she had as a child.

"God, it's freezing! Look at those tiny fish, must be over a hundred."

"Sadly, too small to barbecue." Jen chuckled. "D'you remember bringing our nets here as kids?"

"Yeah, but the coastal rock pools were the best – more creatures to entrap. To be fair, we always let them go afterwards though," said Ava.

"The crabs used to pretend to be dead, and when we released them, they scurried away sideways, like they had dodgy hips, and slid under the pebbles."

Ava laughed. "Yes, I remember."

"Such lovely times," sighed Jen.

A good hour later, they towel-dried wet feet and happily climbed back into the car, bound for their favourite pebbly cove, where a flavoursome picnic of cold pasties, olive salad and coleslaw was readily consumed and more childhood stories animatedly revisited. And come afternoon, a rowing boat, further down the bay, was hired from Joe, the local fisherman, in the hope they might catch cod or pollock for the barbecue.

Ava longed to say that all these activities rendered her happier by far than when she was with Peter, but she thought better of it. She needed, instead, to generate positivity regarding her recent choices, given the already existing animosity between Jen and him. It would be most unwise to mention any misgivings which could well induce Jen to impart yet another lecture apropos the demerits of the man she was moving in with; the man who was, in fact, father to her future child.

"Wow, that's a lot of fish, I'm impressed," declared Abbie, as Ava and Jen strutted proudly down the path, parading the abundant catch in a clear bag. "Let's get the barbecue going."

And, when Ava passed her the haul, she disappeared into the kitchen to prepare the food, while Jen fetched matches to light the fire.

"Yes, we did good," replied Ava, following her mother inside. "We made a great team. The sea got a tad choppy, but otherwise it was fine, stacks of fish for sure."

"I'm glad you had a nice day, darling," smiled Abbie. "So, may I ask when you're moving in with Peter?" she continued, casually changing the subject.

"Soon, I guess. Within the next couple of weeks."

"That'll be a big step."

"Yes," mused Ava. "And I am a little nervous, but it makes perfect sense."

"I completely understand why you would feel unsettled; it's a major change and so soon. Are you sure you're ready?"

Ava glanced reflectively at her mother before she spoke. "Yes, I think so."

"Well, so long as he makes you happy and you like his company, because that's very important."

"I know." There was a pause before she continued. "He's kind to me and keen to do the right thing regarding the baby."

"Would you have moved in with him had you not been pregnant?"

"Probably not just yet," she had to admit. "But I do like him, Mum."

"Like him?"

"OK, love him," she giggled.

At that moment, Jen bounced into the kitchen, thus preventing any further discourse.

"Fire has caught, all good and ready. Can I take anything out?"

"Yes, could you take the salad – oh, and olives,

please?" requested Abbie, slightly distracted as she salted cod and the odd pollock.

"Yep, no problem. Do you know what?" Jen added. "I actually feel I've got a tan, after all that fresh air and sun. How cool is that?"

"You do have a rather healthy outdoor look," agreed Ava, gathering up the bread basket and butter dish and accompanying Jen to the patio, where, in anticipation of receiving the hunter-gatherers' provisions, Abbie had already laid a table. Truth be known, she had also purchased some local fish – just in case, which she now quickly placed in the freezer.

"Wow, this is so succulent! Who needs batter!" piped Jen, masticating with relish as the lemony, fishy fragrance wafted pleasurably into the air, tantalising the tastebuds of floating gulls.

She had, on reflection, decided not to further broach the subject of Ava moving in with Peter. At the end of the day, her friend knew how she felt, and that was enough. So, instead, she relaxed wholeheartedly in the superb company and luxuriated in this perfect evening, as, indeed, did Ava and Abbie.

And far, oh far too soon, they were back on the long road to London and their awaiting reality.

Preparing to Ensnare the Prey

"She's such an utter bitch!" he screamed, saliva sprinkling his lips.

"Who?" said Amanda, a junior employee he had hooked up with for the night.

"Her vile friend, Jen, that's who." And he downed another swig of brandy.

"Well, let's not talk about her now," she said, "otherwise I think I'll leave."

"Oh, yeah, yeah OK, sorry." And he held her firmly in his arms and kissed her, before pushing her down on the bed and roughly tugging off her tights.

"Hey, steady on," she cried, slightly uncomfortable with his wild, unrestrained advances. And he was on her, groaning and grunting, forceful, hungry. But all too soon it was over, and he pulled away, sitting bolt upright on the edge of the bed, leaving her unsatisfied and frustrated.

"I need to sort her out! And Ava! Both of them! I'm in charge, not her – not them!" And he grabbed the brandy bottle and glugged down the remainder of its contents.

"Not this again!" Amanda had had enough of the disagreeable man. "You were supposed to be with me tonight, so you should have bloody well behaved like you wanted to be! I'm going!"

"Not yet, you're not." And he grabbed her throat and pushed her back onto the bed, sprawling on top of her with a terrible force.

"Ow, you're hurting me, get off!" she screamed. "Get off!" And, in a frantic struggle, she sank her teeth hard into his arm, compelling him to let out a cry and instinctively clutch his bleeding limb. In this brief moment, she was up and rushing to the door.

"You say anything about this, and I promise, I'll kill you," he menaced.

Shaking violently, heart racing, she yanked open the door in a wild frenzy, before darting to the temporary sanctum of her room, where she locked the door firmly behind her.

Not one iota of guilt overshadowed Peter the next morning, and his young colleague, who had escaped by the skin of her teeth the previous night, had left the conference by early morning and driven home.

Yesterday's frustration regarding Ava's waywardness, however, had not yet dissolved, leaving him, he decided, with only one obvious option: if he wanted to have more control over her behaviour, more say in her choice of friends, more rights over his future child, he would have to marry the woman, and that was all there was to it. And indubitably, all these requirements could be better achieved via wedlock.

He lay back on the hotel bed, like the cat who got the cream, revelling in a wave of satisfaction over his ingenious ploy.

The Proposal

Ava had left the gym earlier than usual that evening due to a text from Peter, with, untypically, a red heart placed at the end after the words: *I love you*. The message requested she be home at eight since he was preparing a meal.

As this was a relatively rare occurrence, she found herself wondering what exactly had prompted this kind gesture, but far be it for her to delve too deeply and thus destroy the mood. After all, someone else cooking a meal was always a good shout, and after an hour on the treadmill, she had to admit she was famished.

She parked her car, as usual, by the laurel hedge and, deftly dodging the dark-blue berries (messy when punctured) which were scattered like miniature marbles over the paving stones, strode alongside the grass verge, which, currently dotted with bright-coloured dandelions, daisies, and other wildflowers, radiated a veritable meadow-like lustre.

The door was off the latch, as if awaiting her, so she stepped quietly over the threshold and into the long hallway, where a parallel line of chunky, white candles, closely resembling lights on a runway, met her curious gaze. And somewhat fascinated now, she followed the flickering glow – her very own yellow brick road – before veering right and landing in the open doorway of the front room.

Here, she was welcomed by a family of some fifty firefly tapers illuminating the otherwise darkened room, the unequivocal jewel in the crown, however, being tall king and queen cierges poised proudly in dazzling gold on either side of the dining table.

"Wow!" she uttered under her breath.

"Allow me to show you to your table, madam," said Peter, who, appearing out of the shadows, now beckoned.

"It's beautiful," she smiled. "I love it."

"Only the best for you," he replied, elegant in white shirt and black linen trousers, with a Cheshire cat grin spreading like honey over his lips.

"You should have told me to wear something smart."

"Not a problem," he reassured, ushering her to her chair.

After a delectable starter of wild mushroom soup and warm flatbread came the main courses: fresh oysters accompanied by *Mignonette* sauce and *Gim-gui* for Peter, and *Khashlama* for Ava, who marvelled at how considerate he had been in catering so sensitively for her current dietary requirements.

Conversation flowed, helped by the several glasses of champagne he had downed, and when the *crème brûlée* dessert had been consumed, Ava was fit to bursting.

"That was delicious, Peter. Thank you so much."

There was a short pause, before, unable to resist, she casually enquired as to the occasion.

And right on cue, lowering himself onto one knee, he stared lovingly into her eyes, while earnestly offering her a little box inside which lay a rose gold ring, stippled with small diamonds, gleaming like distant stars.

"Will you marry me, Ava?" he asked.

She froze and there ensued a seemingly lengthy pause, the uncertainty of which had started to feel a tad uncomfortable… until tears of joy sprang to her eyes and…

"Yes," she whispered. "Oh, yes."

It had been as easy as that. And *now* she would belong to him.

Wedded Bliss

Several months after the wedding – which had been an unremarkable registry office affair, witnessed only by Ava's mother, who had driven up specially for the ceremony, and Peter's aunt (he had refused point-blank to invite Jen) – Ava had commenced a job in the local florist (on her new husband's insistence), thus leaving her art a peripheral affair, a mere hobby. She had taken his advice in an attempt at keeping a pleasant atmosphere, free of tension and sulks, in the family home.

Arranging flowers was not at all what had been in her mind, but she actually found it quite therapeutic, her boss, Alice, being personable and easy to talk to. So this new path, albeit temporary due to her pregnancy, had proved acceptable after all; although, somewhere deep inside of her, she knew things were not right.

Since the latest investment assistant, a clean-shaven whizz-kid with innovative notions – *absurdly ludicrous* (according to Peter), *he's about twelve, for God's sake!* – had arrived on the scene, her husband had become increasingly irascible, due in part to the newcomer, but also to the company who had left *him*, the previous blue-eyed boy, somewhat overlooked. And the more frequently he felt his proposals being disregarded, the more he took it out on her, with an embittered, fractious tone, until Ava found herself neglected, dismissed, bullied, ever longing for him to air his problems in a healthy, decent manner, thus letting her in.

On a day-to-day basis, there was not a speck of interest demonstrated in her, as if she were invisible, and she so yearned for someone with kindness in their voice, a sparkle in their eyes, and a smile on their lips; maybe even someone to embrace her now and again.

So work had been a blessing in disguise, where she could talk to Alice (an exceedingly good confidant) and thus give vent to these pent-up grievances, this constant churned-up sensation in her chest.

As it had recently become awkward to call from the house (Peter would hover close by, huffing disapproval), Jen was now phoned during breaks and the friends still met up every week at Sweet Retreat, where Ava would paint murals on the walls and take in new pieces of art – created in the privacy of the little hidden room in the attic, which Peter had grudgingly allowed her to occupy.

Needless to say, Jen's friendship had provided her with a steady anchor in an increasingly vulnerable world and their meetings, unbeknown to Peter, had continued well after Isla was born.

Until one day, years later, when Isla was eight, Ava had mentioned Jen's name to her within his hearing, and he had seen red, insisting point-blank that she discontinue any contact, which he maintained was beneficial to neither her nor their child. And that was that. He had spoken. The visits, and phone calls, stopped.

No Justice Served

After suffering depression and self-blame – *she should have left the room earlier, given he was so drunk and angry* – Amanda eventually complained to the manager of the local branch regarding Peter's misconduct towards her, but was strongly advised by Mr Collins that she should take this no further, as the company had had an exemplary record thus far, and such an accusation could well reflect back on her, possibly even impeding her future career, given she was a junior, and Peter many rungs up the ladder. So she remained silent.

Present

Afternoon at the Sanatorium

A sleepy dawn lazily stretched its gilt-orange arms over the horizon, filtering a gentle, golden glow into the dreary guest room via a tiny slit in the centre of the dark satin drapes, causing Isla to blink and rub her drowsy eyes. And a velvet calm flushed through her. Today she would finally be visiting her mother.

For this reason, she jumped out of bed with a rare burst of energy and reached for her pale lemon top and black jeans. Her aunt could say what she wanted regarding her attire; nothing would get to her today. Nothing. And once dressed, she sprinted downstairs to the breakfast room.

"You ought to eat muesli like Peter," nettled Pam in her usual corrosive tones. "Not bread and jam. Biscuits too, I see," she tutted, following Isla's every move. "And that ghastly top again! Really, Isla!"

"Good morning, Aunt," she replied, smiling calmly at the sour-faced woman. "How long before we go?"

"After luncheon, as you well know. Occupy yourself as you wish until then. I have work to do. You could help in the shop, I suppose, or look round the French market down the road, but don't be late back. We eat at 1pm."

By lunchtime, though, anxiety had crept like ivy over Isla's previous peace. She had walked round the bustling market a thousand times, but her mind was overflowing. *Would her mother want to see her? Would she be drugged up, like Father said?* It was the not knowing that had a grip on her. But at least she had managed to find a cute little painted-wood robin in one of the stalls, which she felt sure Ava would love. And for this she was grateful.

Virtual silence prevailed over the dinner table. Mounting expectation merging with a stomach already full of butterflies meant she could barely swallow the food on her plate. Father was clearly preoccupied, probably with work, as he chewed on his lamb cutlet, and Aunt was quieter than earlier, which was a blessing.

The clock's tick-tock, tick-tock eventually gave way to a loud chime inducing her heart to race. And then came the signal she had been waiting for all morning.

"Right," said Father, gulping down his water. "Have you got everything? We need to make a move. Get this over with. Remember, Isla, you won't be staying long. I'll wait outside in the car park, like we agreed."

"Yes, Father," she replied, restlessly grabbing her bag before darting like lightning to the car.

And the reassuring rumble of the engine was music to her ears.

The elaborate facade of the sanatorium faced her with brazen superiority; no doubt her father had opted for the most exclusive institution. And she shivered inadvertently before glancing at her hard, expressionless aunt, an unwelcome personal guard, who towered over her, cradling the latest designer handbag tenderly under her arm, like a diamond-collared trophy dog.

"Well, come on, Isla. Let's get this unpleasant affair over with. I haven't got all day," she snapped, marching purposefully towards the grand entrance, and firmly twisting the hefty brass handle on the oak-panelled doors.

Like a stray cat, the child followed, nervous and out of place as she tentatively stepped into the lavishly bedecked, germ-free reception area.

"Good afternoon." The receptionist whiffed of an excessive dose of top-end *parfum* as she simpered insincerely through rouge, recently collagened lips. "Yes, of course, Mrs Mills is waiting for you," she drawled in a gratingly self-important voice. "Ensure you sign the visitor's book and then go down the hall and turn first right."

Isla approached and shakily scrawled her name. *But wait.* Bouncing off the page with irreversible finality was the same surname as hers – Mills – Peter Mills – several lines up from her own signature and, on further inspection, her father's name appeared on previous pages too! *It couldn't be!* Yet the stark evidence of his visits lay before her very eyes in black and white.

However, now hearing her aunt's irritated and impatient call echoing distantly in her head, she managed, from somewhere deep inside, to quell the turmoil of such a betrayal before numbly trailing behind, like unwanted baggage, to the visitor's lounge.

Perched like a shadow, hopelessly lost in the all-consuming arms of a plush, padded chair, was Mother, her faded-green eyes staring vacantly into space.

"Well, here she is," said her aunt, sotto voce. "The mother you were so desperate to see. Just look at her – what a sorry state," she added, tone like gravel underfoot.

Hearing indistinct voices, Ava turned, a swift twitch of a smile visiting her lips as she beheld her daughter, which transformed, quick as a sting, to a hurt, pallid gaze on noting the presence of Pam.

And it was due to witnessing this exact moment in time that Isla suddenly swung round to her aunt, a strange surge of determination and courage colouring her cheeks.

"You need to go. Now. My mother doesn't want you here and neither do I. Wait in the car with Father. Go. Now."

The words, which seemed to come from someone else, were expressed with a quiet, yet conclusive, surety. And utterly taken aback, the woman, snarling in a barely audible voice that Peter would hear of this, brusquely exited the room.

Isla fell into her mother's arms with an intense urgency and clung on for dear life, wishing to stay in this beautiful embrace for all eternity.

"Oh Isla, darling, you came," cried Ava. "I phoned, but Peter said you didn't have time to see me, that you were too busy, with schoolwork, clubs and friends, to visit."

"No, no! That's simply not true! Not how it was at all. I've missed you so much. I didn't have your number. When will you be coming home? It's awful without you, just awful."

"I don't know yet. I feel tired every day. So very tired. The tablets they give make me terribly drowsy, but Peter says I need to stay. He doesn't want me upsetting you."

"Oh, Mum. You could never do that, never! I need you. You must get better. You must. I need you." And silent teardrops trickled down her now-pale cheeks and onto her sad lips.

"Isla, dear, how beautiful you are; that soft-yellow top suits you… reminds me of the primroses and buttercups in Granny's garden. But I've let you down. I'm sorry."

"It's not your fault, Mum."

"Everything's so hard to deal with, Isla. I'm not well."

"But you will get better. This is only temporary."

"I do hope so, darling. Is Marmalade OK?"

"Yes, he's fine; he's invaluable company. I have a present," she continued, handing her mother the little robin. "I hope you like it."

"Oh, it's lovely, thank you." And Ava burst into tears.

"Don't cry, Mum," consoled Isla, gently holding her hand. "I'm here. I'll always be here."

There was a brief pause before she spoke again. "I wanted to ask – does Granny know? Only she hasn't called us in ages."

"No, she doesn't," replied Ava in a whisper. "Peter thought it best."

"He told me she had gone to stay with her sister; and he refused to bring me here or give me your number because he said you were drugged up and wouldn't even know me, let alone want to talk."

"Oh dear, oh dear!" she exclaimed, vigorously chewing her lower lip. "What's happening? Why would he say that? I don't feel very well. It's too much. All of it. Too much. Where's Jen? I miss her."

Gradually remembering a woman of that name from her younger days, Isla recalled being taken to a small café, on Saturdays, for milkshake and muffin, but these afternoons out seemed to have become few and far between over time until they tailed off completely.

"Do you mean Jen… from that little café with homemade cakes and your pictures on the wall?"

"Jen, yes, that's right, the very one! Oh, you remember!" cried Ava, relief lighting up her features. "It's called Sweet Retreat – near Camden town. I loved taking you there."

"Of course I remember; but why did we stop going?"

"Peter didn't approve…" she murmured, her voice barely audible. "But you'd better go now, darling, I'm just so very tired. Please come back when you can. I shall wait for you. Every day I'll wait."

"I promise," replied Isla, kissing her mother on the cheek. But her thoughts were riddled with conflict as she reluctantly returned to the car park.

"Get in," hissed her father. "We'll talk when we get home. I knew this was a mistake."

Her aunt was silent.

The trees along the highway formed a blur of smudged watercolours, flimsily merging with chubby hedgerows, which spanned out to a cloud-blotched sky, faintly beheld through the weary lenses of her tear-stained eyes.

So many lies. Such vile deceit. *How could he?*

"How many times did you visit without telling me?" she asked through gritted teeth. "*How many?*"

"I *said* we'll talk when we get home!"

"You told her I was too busy to see her," she sobbed, her shallow breaths like hiccups. "You said I didn't want to talk to her! *You said—*"

"Be quiet! I told you I will *not* discuss it here! Not now!"

"Did *she* know?" continued Isla, wildly pointing at her aunt with a feverish fervour. "*Did she?*"

"I most certainly did not, you stupid girl! And I'm telling you, young lady, your rudeness shall not be forgiven in a hurry. I've *never* been spoken to in such a way in my entire life!"

"You deserved it," Isla muttered, wiping her eyes.

"I said *enough!*" he thundered so violently as to quash any further discourse.

And for the rest of the journey, a blanket of murky darkness smothered them.

The Next Day

"I merely wanted to protect you, Isla. You'll understand one day. Your mother is not the right person to have around at the moment; she's a bad influence."

"She's my mother, I need her – and you went to see her on numerous occasions and fed her with lies about me – lied to me about *her* too."

"I didn't want you seeing her, Isla – simple as that. She'll be home when she's well and there's an end to it."

"Well, I'm going to visit. I'll catch a bus, now I know where she's staying."

"No, Isla, you'll do no such thing. I forbid it. Your exams are fast approaching and you need to revise; so, each day you'll come straight home, and that's the end of it. If you disobey me, young lady, I swear I'll lock you in your room. Oh, and you'll apologise to your aunt when she next comes over. Your behaviour was despicable."

Isla stayed silent, realising there was no way of getting through to her father. It was pointless attempting to reason with him. He had to be in charge, in control of everyone, everything – no matter what.

But she had already decided what her next move would be, and no one would stop her. *No one.*

Creative Writing Class

"That was extremely poignant. Well done, Emily. Right, so next up is Isla Mills. When you're ready."

And, walking tentatively to the front of the class with paper in hand, Isla started to read. She had had neither time nor the inclination to prepare anything, what with the weekend events, so had quickly scribbled her poem on the bus in.

The Butterfly

My mother flew from tree to tree, a butterfly like me
She spread her fragile bright-blue wings
So happy to be free.

But while at rest on a buttercup, a slimy toad stood by
It opened its mouth and snapped her up
As I watched, I could but sigh.

So, whatever you do, be careful
Learn from the butterfly's plight
Watch your back, don't trust a soul
Or you could be dead tonight.

"Thank you, Isla. A very different style to Emily's. Interesting. What is the message here, class? Daniel?"

"Not to sit on buttercups, Miss."

The class laughed.

Isla clicked her tongue. "Moron," she muttered under her breath.

Shortly the bell sounded, triggering a reflex reaction as students began gathering books, pens, manically flinging them into open rucksacks as they waited, like caged bears, desperate for their release.

"Ems!" called Isla as her friend darted out of the door and down the corridor. "Wait for me!"

On hearing her name, Emily stopped and spun round.

"I need a favour," said Isla, rushing to catch up. "Could I borrow your phone for a moment to check an address?"

"God, haven't you got one yet?"

"No, my dad doesn't think it necessary."

"That's stupid, everyone needs a phone! Is he Amish or something?"

"No, *he* has one. Who knows, he might finally come round and buy me one on my sixteenth?"

"Here's hoping! But don't be long, I've got choir practice, like *now*."

"'K." And awkwardly tapping the keys, she managed to scan a map of coffee shops in the Camden area, handing back the mobile just a few minutes later.

"Thanks."

"No worries."

"I liked your poem, by the way."

"Yeah – yours too." Emily grinned. "How long did it take to write?"

"I believe in concision. It's not about length, but quality," informed Isla with mock seriousness. "Take haikus… and I rest my case."

"*Interesting…*" replied her friend, mimicking the teacher's words. "Anyhow, got to go. See you tomorrow."

"Yeah, bye for now."

And, fuelled with excitement and anticipation, Isla sprinted out into the open air, turning purposefully in the opposite direction to home.

A wild sense of liberation grasped her as she strolled through the market, inhaling the flavours of freshly fried samosas and breathing in the scent of multi-toned, perfumed candles. She lost herself in the light clouds of aromata, enticing balms, exotic spices, and stroked fresh linen and fine silks, marvelling at the textures and vivid hues highlighted by the warm rays of a newly present sun. The sweet, fragrant citrus of squeezed oranges wafted through her nostrils, well-nigh impossible to resist; even the pungent smell of raw fish and hanging leather earned a place in this noisy, vibrant corner of the city.

But swiftly made aware of her mission by a rosy-cheeked woman tugging at her child to hurry or they'd be late, she strode down the street, leaving the busy rumble of Camden Lock behind her.

Along several winding roads she walked, only stopping once to ask directions, until before long the tiny café appeared as large as life in front of her, leaning affectionately against a neglected, but still-dignified, Victorian building. And there it was: *Sweet Retreat* in hand-painted, pink and gold writing.

Taking a deep breath, she opened the door and peered into the room, like an intrigued yet cautious cat. All around her, Ava's painted murals still adorned the whitewashed walls, bathed in a carnival of dancing colours – floating, fluffy, weightless; rainbow-curls, swirls, silken sunsets, velvet moonshine. Embracing, lifting. No angles, no hard edges, just flowing, frothing, foamy waves.

"How beautiful," she reflected, smiling proudly.

Shortly she moved to a red chair at a turquoise table, and waited until a young, fresh-faced waitress surfaced.

"Can I help you?"

"I'd like a flat white, please. And do you know if Jen's around today?"

"Yes, she's out the back on a break. Shall I get her for you?"

"No, it's OK, don't disturb her. I'll have a drink first and wait here."

"Sure. Would you like a cake?"

"Do you know what, forget the coffee, I'll have a strawberry milkshake and a blueberry muffin," she said, basking in the beating heart of this warm, cosy place.

"Chrissie, I need to water those geraniums. Remind me, please; I'll get on to it later," called Jen, coming through the back door.

"OK, will do. There's someone waiting for you on table five, by the way. Wanted a chat when you came off your break."

"You should have said."

"She told me she was fine to wait."

"Alright then, thanks."

On approaching table five, Jen opened her eyes wide in disbelief.

"Isla," she whispered. "What are the odds?"

"You recognised me," came the surprised reply. "It was years ago. How did you know?"

"Your signature order of strawberry milkshake and blueberry muffin gave me a clue – was always your favourite." She smiled. "Then your lovely dimples… how could I forget those? And your dark blonde hair; you look the same, just older. You're so like your mother." And she hugged the girl tightly. "How wonderful to see you. How *is* Ava?"

"Actually, she's the reason I'm here; I need to talk to you, Jen. To ask your advice."

"OK. Let's go somewhere quieter. Follow me. Chrissie! I'll be upstairs for a while. Hold the fort, please."

"Will do."

And, climbing the spiral staircase, they found themselves in a snug little room where they sank into the softness of a saffron-yellow sofa embellished with red, calico cushions.

"Right, I'm all ears," encouraged Jen. "But before you start, your mum's OK, isn't she? She's not ill or anything."

"She's in a sanatorium in the hills about nine miles from us," replied Isla, tears welling up in her eyes. "She's had a breakdown."

Jen nodded sadly and her brow furrowed as she gently reached for the tissues. "You'd best start from the beginning, sweetheart. Tell me everything. I've all the time in the world."

Arriving home at 8pm – Jen had given her a lift – Isla was exhausted yet happy. Happy to have shared her story, thereby diluting some of her angst, but, most importantly, having imparted it to a dear, trusted friend of Ava's made her feel safe.

Luckily her father was not around, or he would, doubtless, have questioned her lateness.

Mounting the stairs two by two, hopeful that the downward spiral would, after today, rapidly change direction, she slipped on her pyjamas, grabbed a book, and jumping into bed, was welcomed by her warm, purring cushion coiled up under the covers like a snail in its shell.

Isla's Birthday

A bright sun playfully bounced into the pale-blue skies as the special Saturday eventually emerged. Isla was now sixteen, although often she felt much, much older. Yet today, a cheerful exuberance embraced her. This was, in part, due to Father being absent for the entire weekend at yet another *conference*; although, given the recent frequency of these meetings, Isla suspected him of having an affair, and his mellower moods, as well as the faint whiff of a woman's fragrance on his coat, supported her suspicion.

The main reason, however, for the spritely spring in her step was because today she would be visiting her mother. Jen had explained everything on the landline the night before and was to pick her up in the early afternoon. So Isla was eagerly counting the hours until her imminent arrival.

The plan was to rescue Ava.

A cake had been sent by the girl's aunt with *Happy Birthday* written in glaring pink on a hideously tasteless icing base smothered in ghastly violet and red balloons; these were held by creepy-looking elves with questionably wide, nefarious grins. And even though Isla had fleetingly entertained the notion that it may well be laced with deadly nightshade, she had soon deemed it safe to eat, in the knowledge that her father would, almost certainly, partake of a slice at some point during the week – a fact which Pam surely knew – and, quite frankly, her aunt would never have bothered to make one herself anyway!

A card, too, had been left for her on the kitchen table with, ironically, a picture of a gift box tied with colourful ribbon – there *was* no present, but instead, a stained fifty-pound note had been tossed haphazardly into the envelope. The only words were: *Happy Birthday.* No name, no kisses, no message apart from the one hitherto printed on the card itself. She had asked Father for a mobile, but the answer had, as expected, been, "No. Maybe next year. They're a distraction. You don't need one yet."

Lunch had been a lone ginger biscuit dunked into her third cup of tea, yet she was bursting with energy and when the bell rang, she bolted to the door like a marathon runner vying for first place.

"Hello, sweetheart," piped Jen, cheerily handing over a small parcel, while singing, "Happy birthday to you, happy birthday to you…"

"Thank you so much!" Isla giggled, excitedly tearing open the packaging. "Oh… wow!" she whispered when she saw the gift, and there were tears in her eyes. "It's wonderful. Thank you, thank you!" And, clasping the mobile phone in her hand, she hugged Jen with the enormity of an affectionate bear.

"It's a pleasure, darling. But maybe best not mention it to your dad. Keep it under lock and key."

"Oh, yes, I most certainly will. Thank you, Jen, I love it!"

"You're finally connected to the outside world," she smiled. "Right then, no time to waste. Grab your coat and we'll go rescue your mum!"

Fading Away

Slumped like a deflated Li-lo on the thickly padded, high-legged armchair, lay Ava, silently staring into a pastel-coloured, all-too-solid space, which hemmed her in, sewed her up like burlap. Soon, though, her meds would sneak like thieves in the night, dulling her despondency; and the stark metal edges of objects – doors, tables, the doctor's glasses – along with the noise and clatter of teacups being mechanically cleared away by overly smiley staff, would dissolve into gaseous swirls and float round the gloomy, germ-free room, rubbing out the truth.

And this blurry world, which blotted out a stabbing reality and hid her in the depths of nothingness, was one she now inhabited.

But if ever the chemical effects wore off, an acute clarity would sweep painfully through her mind, brushing away the dizzy dust.

"You don' t need friends, Ava; you have me. We'll go to the shops together and I'll help you choose an outfit for my office party... and don't talk to anyone about the plates I smashed... or the bruises; everyone has problems,

Ava, but it's our business, no one else's." He made her think his subtle commands were her own ideas. "*It's good you decided not to see Jen anymore. She was a bad influence, you're well rid.*" But, in truth, she' d had no choice; she feared him. "*Poor Ava, I know you try your best. I'll look after you.*" And he had patted her head as if she were a dog.

She'd forgotten how to smile over the years, and the taut, inflexible muscles round her lips formed a tight line which simply would not curl upwards, leaving her dead, as if numbed by a venomous snake or Botox injection.

How had she managed before? Her wide grin had appeared effortlessly, had it not? Was she poor, pathetic, like he'd said? And that's why Isla didn't love her anymore, he'd told her. "*She' s moved on, Ava. She has a new life; she doesn't need you anymore.*" Had she screamed then? Had she…?

"Shh… your medication is due, Ava. Take these." A patronisingly soft voice accompanied the two white and yellow capsules. "You'll feel calmer in a bit. We don't want you disturbing the others now, do we."

On the cusp of oblivion settling in, she recalled creating an Easter bonnet with a four-year-old Isla, who had proudly marched with her to the kitchen to show Pam. However, far from praise for their efforts, all they had received was a derisive huff and a toss of the head, before the woman had purposefully exited the room.

"*Tell his aunt to go screw herself!*" Jen had said when Ava told her how upset she and Isla had been.

"*It's not that easy,*" had come the sad reply.

Afternoon with Ava

For the second time, Isla was driven into the car park of the sanatorium, with tyres scraping discordantly against the textured paving stones.

"I feel a little sick," she confessed.

"No need," replied Jen. "Trust me; all will be fine. Just give it time."

Isla nodded and a weak smile formed on her lips.

"I called your granny and she's driving up as we speak."

"Thank goodness."

"Yes. By the end of the day, Ava will be on her way to Cornwall; you just wait and see. Your mother can leave this place whenever she chooses; she can go today as long as a family member takes her – and that's where Abbie comes in. So don't worry."

"You make it sound so simple," sighed Isla.

"And why shouldn't it be?"

She shrugged.

"Come on, girl," asserted Jen purposefully. "Wield all the courage you can muster into your gait, your demeanour. Let's jump out of the car and save Ava!"

And the steadfast duo, holding this pressing mission close to their hearts, marched determinedly into the reception hall to sign the visitors' book.

"Gosh, feels like we're visiting royalty," whispered Jen as they traversed the overembellished foyer.

"I know, it's not very cosy… Jen?"

"Yes, dear."

"Should we write our actual names? What if Father comes? He'll go mad if he finds out we've visited without his permission."

"Of course we'll put our actual names. *Let* him find out. He's a bully. You've got to do your own thing and stand up to him."

"Ha-ha! Easier said than done. You don't live with him. He can be scary."

"Then we need to break the mould – together. Ready?"

"Ready."

But as she thrust open the swing door into the lounge area where guests were received, Jen could not prevent a sudden, sharp intake of breath as she spotted her poor, defeated friend.

Heavily sunken into the exaggerated layers of padding on the oversized chair and bleary-eyed from her last meds, with a glazed expression further benumbing her already still face, Ava stared blankly at the pastel walls, as yet unaware of anyone's presence.

"We need to get some coffee down her," suggested Jen.

"Yes. Shall I fetch some?" ventured Isla sadly.

"God, it's so sterile in here, these awful beige walls

would drive me crazy, make me want to tear my hair out! It could most certainly do with a selection of your mother's art, that's for sure. Shall we try and sell them some?" And a strained smile touched her lips.

"I think the rooms are neutral in order to keep patients calm," replied Isla, glumly gazing at her mother.

"Well our Ava certainly looks calm! But I think that's the meds, don't you?"

"Is she asleep?"

"No, her eyes are open. Yes, pop and get coffee, sweetheart, and I'll pinch her hard." She forced a grin.

Ava smiled vacuously to herself as Jen approached. But, as the footsteps neared, a contorted tremor momentarily replaced her prior vacancy. *"I promise I'll stay – do everything you say. Please don't tell Isla I'm crazy. Tell her I love her. I love her. Oh dear, what's happening…what's happening?"* And her muffled tones took on a shrill ring.

"It's OK, darling, it's Jen, your old friend. Don't fret, sweetheart; all will be fine, trust me." And she tried to mask her shock at Ava's emaciated frame.

"Jen…?"

"The one and only." She stroked Ava's hair before cupping the wan face gently in her hands. And instinctively Ava gripped her in a tight, desperate embrace.

"Wow! I couldn't have hoped for a better welcome!" she chuckled. "Steady now, you're going to crush me."

"I'm sorry…" came the whispered response, in another flash of effortless lucidity. "So sorry."

"I get it, it's fine," reassured Jen. "I'm here now and that's all that matters."

Nudging open the double doors, Isla neared, hurriedly handing the coffee to Jen, before rushing to her mother's side.

"Mum!"

"Oh, my darling child; is it really you? Did he let you come after all? Where is he?"

Isla shot a forlorn glance at Jen who, deftly suppressing her rage, assisted Ava with her coffee.

"Drink this and you'll feel clearer," she urged. "We need to talk."

Like a child, Ava sipped the strong coffee, every now and then glancing up at her friend and over at her daughter to ensure they were really there.

"How do you feel now?" asked Jen after Ava had swallowed the last of the caffeine.

"I feel tired… *dead* tired."

"You need to be out of here, that's why. This place is no good. All you're having is copious amounts of drugs pumped into you."

"Because I'm not well," came the mumbled reply.

"But, darling, these drugs are no solution. Sitting on your own all day is no solution. Surely you can see that."

"Peter told me I have to stay here until I am fit to go home. But he said it will take many months and I must be patient."

"Listen, Ava," replied Jen, inwardly infuriated by the words of the odious man. "Your mum is driving up today and she – well, all of us – think you should go back to Cornwall with her to convalesce. Trust me, this isn't the right environment, but I think you know that already. You won't recover here; you'll just get worse. What do you think?"

"Oh, thank you – but I can't. Peter said—"

"Ava, he wants you out of the way," interrupted her friend, struggling with her wrath. "*He* is keeping you here, filling your mind with lies. Look at me; you need to get out, not only for your sake, but your daughter's too."

A silent, contorted pain spread over the woman's face, and she struggled not to cry.

"Abbie will look after you, darling. She'll care for you until you are well; trust me, this is your chance to get better, to be free. Please listen to me, sweetheart. You know we only want the best for you. And I'm sorry to say, Peter doesn't; he just wants power over you and the more confused and dependent you are, the stronger he feels."

"Oh dear," she murmured, anxiously chewing her lower lip. "Oh dear…"

"Mum, listen to Jen," implored Isla, unable to contain her distress any longer. "I beg you."

A painful quiet commanded the room. Nothing more was said, and when tea and cake were brought in for Ava and her visitors, no one ate a thing.

The arrival of Abbie just a short while later saw the three women slumped glumly in the cream, faux-leather, memory-foam chairs. Persuading Ava hadn't been as easy as Jen had anticipated. Mistakenly, she had assumed her friend would be eager to escape to freedom, yet Peter's words were far too ingrained in her mind for this plan to be at all straightforward.

"Hi all!" exclaimed Abbie with forced jollity as she breezed up to them pretending not to notice Ava's pale, agitated countenance. "So lovely to see you, darling," she continued, hugging her daughter's frail frame a tad too tightly, prompting Ava to wince before yielding, while her sombre eyes highlighted her turmoil.

"Granny!" cried Isla, eagerly jumping up for a hug.

"Hello, sweetheart. Happy Birthday." Her words were almost silent as she gently pressed a turquoise ring into Isla's hand. And understanding this sensitive gesture – executed solely to shield Ava from realising she had forgotten the day – Isla mouthed, "Thank you, I love it." And Abbie wrapped her arms affectionately round her granddaughter, before adding, "Your mother and I will be travelling to Cornwall today, did Jen tell you?"

"Yes, Granny, but Mum doesn't want to go," replied Isla sadly.

"She will, just give me a bit of time with her," whispered Abbie. "Maybe you two could go and grab a coffee?" she suggested, smiling at Jen. "There's a café just five minutes up the road; I saw it as I drove here."

"Good idea. We could do with a bit of fresh air," answered Jen, putting her arm around Isla. "Come on, let's go."

"Give us an hour or so; that should suffice," reassured Abbie in as calm a voice as she could muster.

Jen nodded in accordance and the pair disappeared in the blink of an eye, leaving the double doors still swinging.

The warm sun embraced them as they emerged

from the air-conditioned, windowless room, which had enveloped them like an airtight pod – a sterile, featureless dimension, shut off from the real world. And they strolled arm-in-arm along the sun-drenched pavement, grateful to have escaped this oppressive cell, albeit for an hour.

"Some of those poor 'clients' resemble zombies in many ways, except, of course, for their designer clothes and impeccable hairdos – so depressing! It made me think of *The Stepford Wives*," commented Jen, but noting Isla's blank expression, she set about explaining the chilling context.

"Sounds awful. It was a horror film, right?"

"Hell, yes! Do you even have to ask?" And they laughed out loud, which helped channel their nervous tension.

"Don't worry, sweetheart; if anyone can persuade your mum to leave, it's your grandmother," she said. "Have faith."

Abbie cradled her daughter in her arms without saying a word. She stroked her hair tenderly, rubbed her back; she held her hands, her actions generating warmth, compassion. And they remained in this state of quietude until she felt Ava's heart beat more slowly and her previously tense body, despite constant medication, nestle steadily into hers. And she sang – a song she used to sing to Ava in her childhood – softly, softly reassuring, and soothing, holding her constantly in a gentle embrace. Memories were revisited in whispers, flushing through the girl's body like a warm, consoling breeze – stories of the sea, picnics in the dunes, skipping through fields of wildflowers, evening barbecues, siestas, swinging softly in the hammock attached to two elderly oaks, staring up at the stars. Uncomplicated, magical. And Ava was a child again.

An hour later, when Jen and Isla returned, Abbie told them that Ava had agreed to go home with her and asked them to tell the receptionist to prepare the documentation for her discharge. This they did instantly, with speed and efficiency, for fear there might be a change of heart, but there was none. Ava's room was cleared, her personal items packed neatly in an eagerly awaiting case, proof of Abbie's identity checked, consent forms signed, signatures firmly written on the dotted line, a week's medication provided… And the hugely relieved women, with firm arms round Ava's shoulders, strode swiftly past the reception desk, followed by the receptionist's expressionless eyes and insincere, collagen-lipped smirk, to the exit, where, after vigorously twisting the cold, brass knob, they marched tenaciously through the oak-panelled doors for the very last time, and out into the welcoming sunlight.

Work Experience

"Pam says wear something smart, Isla. White blouse and black skirt," said Peter. "And put your hair up, in a bun or something."

"Bun?" she questioned. "Why can't I wear it loose?"

"It's about creating the correct impression, Isla. Her clients are rich and influential; they expect staff to be elegant, sophisticated."

"OK. I'll do my best," she replied, determined to make the most of a far from ideal situation.

"Good, don't let her down. I'll take you over in an hour."

"Do I need to prepare a packed lunch?"

"Not a clue, Isla." *Did she discern irritation in his voice?* Strange, after all these years, that she was still affected by it, that it still caused a dull ache. "She'll probably provide lunch," he continued, oblivious of her dejected mien. "Failing that you can go to a café; use your common sense. Now, get ready, and hurry."

And, instantly distracted by this new challenge, she turned on her heel, striding the stairs two at a time to work on her transformation.

Why didn't he say anything when she returned in her full regalia: pencil skirt, white blouse, neat bun with thin-black ribbon – even a small clutch bag and short black blazer? Everything he had asked for! Why did he just glance at her briefly and then get up? Why? Couldn't he have just said: *You look nice, Isla*?

But alas, his only words were: "Come on then, let's go. Don't want to be late on your first day."

And downcast, she followed him to the car.

Halfway through the silent journey, however, she reflected that he would doubtless have said something unkind had she *not* looked good, so him remaining silent must surely mean she *did* look good, and in this new reasoning she took solace.

"Right," he stated curtly as he pulled into the private car park. "We're here. I'll come back at 5.30pm; we'll have dinner at Pam's and then home."

"OK. See you later, Father."

"Yes." And, without another word, he drove off into the distance.

Even though the sun was shining brightly, a shiver flushed through her as she pressed the bell, and she wished she could be anywhere but here.

After a minute or so, her aunt appeared and led her into the musty-smelling building.

"So, are you ready to start?" she stated matter-of-factly, while looking Isla up and down with fixed scrutiny. And again, it was wearisome to decipher whether her aunt was displeased or, rather, found her chosen outfit agreeable, so she decided to apply the same logic as she had in the car regarding her father's reactions.

"Yes, I'm ready," came the brave reply. And she followed the obnoxious woman through the sliding doors and into the shop, preparing to meet her indubitable fate.

The show room, which embraced an elegant, if somewhat aloof, ambience, afforded ample space to accommodate all her aunt's treasures. Glass display cases, casually leaning at a forty-five degree angle, lined the lower section of the long glass countertop, housing several pieces of antique jewellery, which, according to Pam, were highly sought after by anyone with money and discerning taste.

A few Victorian vases and porcelain figures from the same period were dotted along the walls on marble plinths, quietly awaiting a home. And a vintage mahogany cash register, latterly adapted for cards, nestled comfortably on the edge of the glass surface, eager, in its greedy anticipation, to be fed copious amounts of money throughout the course of the day.

"So, go and make us a cup of coffee, Isla," said Pam eventually, after waxing lyrical regarding all her priceless chattels. "One sugar for me, and then I'll show you where the cleaning equipment is, and you can get started on polishing the display cases. I'll guide you through all your chores – oh, and the tiles need mopping after that. So hurry up. Bring me a stem ginger biscuit as well. In the cupboard."

"But Aunt!" Isla protested, feeling she should change her name to Cinderella. "I dressed up to come here. Father said… I just assumed I'd be working in the shop."

"First lesson, Isla dear. Never assume anything."

"When is my lunch break?" she ventured grudgingly.

"That's not the attitude, Isla. You need to demonstrate enthusiasm and willingness. And if you want a good report from me, you'll have to earn it."

"Yes, Aunt. But where can I buy lunch – *when* the time comes?" she quietly persisted.

Pam tutted disapprovingly. "There's a café just outside and a bakery as well. If you have time for a break, you may go to the café, if not you can grab something from the bakery and bring it back here to eat."

Isla sighed deeply before making for the kitchen to commence her day of drudgery in this veritable purgatory.

Of course, there was not time enough for a proper break, such was her toil, so she popped into the bakery and returned to devour a baguette in the kitchen.

In the afternoon, multiple purchases were made by well-dressed men and women with drawlingly ostentatious accents; and Isla was surprised, as she fetched celebratory champagne which she poured carefully into thin crystal flutes, that the cash register didn't have dyspepsia.

And at 5.30pm on the dot, her father arrived. *Did he ask how her day had gone?* Of course not. Did Pam thank her for her help? No. Nothing. So why on earth did she feel sad? When would she learn not to expect kindness? When?

Halfway through their evening meal, and as if Isla wasn't there, her father turned to Pam and asked, "So, how was she?"

"A little sulky, if you want the truth, but otherwise not too bad," gloated Pam with a malignant pleasure.

"Well, I'm sure you'll have a more positive attitude tomorrow, won't you, Isla?" he replied sternly.

"But Father, I dressed up, like you said, and all I did was clean and fetch drinks."

"You have to start from the bottom," chimed her aunt jarringly.

"Yes, but I'm only here for a week, I'm hardly going to rise to the upper echelons."

"Enough!" said Peter, anger seeping into his voice. "You are very lucky to have been given this opportunity. Be grateful."

"Yes," she replied, seething inside. How she hated them both!

And, oh, how the week dragged with the tedious tasks and her aunt's constant admonishments! Did she learn anything about sales, or the history and value of antiques? No. Nothing. Did she converse with or serve any customers? No. None. Unless, of course, you consider the delivering of top-end bubbly and vol-au-vents stuffed with caviar to all the parvenus and moneyed entrepreneurs; for every sizeable sale was followed by a toast and canapés. And it vexed Isla no end to witness her aunt's charming demeanour around customers, her amicable dialogue, her effortless quips – such a contrast to the way in which she spoke to her.

But, even after a long and dreary day, on returning to the privacy of her room, peace could not be found. A hideous dread clenched her insides as she imagined her father finding out that Ava was no longer at the sanatorium, but in Cornwall with Abbie. And learning of his daughter's subterfuge would, no doubt, drive him insane; she could already envisage, with acute horror, his crazed look, and, frankly, her angst, in the knowledge that he could very well kill her, threw the poor child into a state of delirium. Thank God for her mobile; she could at least call for help if needed, and, because of Jen, was able to phone Ava every day, which was a huge comfort for mother and child alike.

"*Don't worry, Isla,*" explained Jen when the girl related her concerns. "*Just tell Peter it was all my idea. And give him my phone number. He will definitely ring! If this doesn't work, I'll come round at the first sign of any trouble, I promise. Let me know immediately, OK?*"

"*OK. Thanks, Jen. I'm just relieved Mum is with Granny. And she seems calmer now when I talk to her. I can't wait to go and visit.*"

"*Well, you'll have to be patient on that score. Take things slowly.*"

"*Yes, understood. And I'll happily wait now I know she's in safe hands.*"

"*Good. And make sure you get plenty of sleep before your final day of enslavement with the Wicked Witch of the West.*"

"*Will do,*" she laughed. "*Goodnight. Speak tomorrow.*"

"*Yes. Night, sweetheart.*"

And, much reassured, Isla slipped under the covers, soon to be joined by a soft, thermic ball of purring ginger.

The Cat Leaps Out of the Bag

Funnily, it was soon after Isla had voiced her concerns to Jen that Peter actually deigned to visit Ava in the sanatorium. He reasoned he had nowhere more pressing to go that evening, so he might as well, if only for the sport of it.

And exhibiting a phlegmatic, purposeful gait, he entered the establishment, paced over to the reception desk and, with more than a hint of salaciousness, leered at the collagen-lipped pout of the receptionist, who readily reciprocated this inappropriate gesture.

"Hi, how are you today? Looking good," he gushed. And she offered an inveigling smile. "Shall I go through? Oh, wait, I'll sign in first."

"Um, I thought you knew," she said, somewhat bewildered. "Mrs Mills discharged herself – just recently."

"What?" he hissed. "That can't be right. Are you sure you're not mixing her up with someone else?"

"Perfectly sure. Her mother came to collect her."

"Her mother?" He stared at her, aghast.

"Yes, and your daughter came – and another woman – a friend, I think she said."

"A friend?"

"Yes."

"Who?"

"Sorry?"

"I said, *who*?" And his raised voice made her gasp.

"Jen," she replied after sulkily checking the book.

"*Bitch*," he growled under his breath.

"What?"

"Oh, nothing. Thanks. I'd better go now," he muttered, his face livid. "I need to sort this out." And turning, without so much as an alluring wink, he stormed out of the building to his car.

Isla was studying in her room when her father returned, but the front door was thrown open so forcefully that it flew into the side table, knocking over a ceramic vase, thus prompting him to spit out a stream of abuse. On hearing the commotion, she jumped up and opened her bedroom door a crack, in order to gauge what was happening.

Harsh, rasping tones reached the top of the stairs, and she shuddered.

"Isla! Isla!" came an awful voice. "Get down here this minute! And hurry!"

"Coming, Father."

She put on her shoes and, flustered and uneasy, rushed down to the kitchen, where her father was pouring a large whiskey.

"What the hell, Isla!" he shouted. "I've just been to

the sanatorium, and they told me that your mother has left – gone down to Cornwall with your gran – and that you were there! With *Jen*! Now, you explain this to me right away, young lady!"

Isla stood still, frantically wondering if now would be a good time to sprint up the stairs, lock her door and phone Jen, but somehow, she stayed put.

"Y… yes, I did go with Jen to see Mum, it's true," she stammered. "The sanatorium was making her worse. She needed to be with Granny by the sea – at home."

"At home? This is her home!" he bellowed.

"No, it's not! You sent her away and told her to stay away. And she got worse in that place, drugged up all the time."

"I did what was best for her, Isla," he said, a tad less raucously. "Can't you see that?"

"No. You did what was best for you. Not Mum. Not me. So I went to see Jen and told her everything, and she contacted Granny."

"*Jen!*" he yelled. "Always that bloody interfering bitch!"

"She's not!" cried Isla. "She's kind and she loves Mum and me – *unlike you*!" And she sobbed fiercely into her arm.

"Get to your room, ungrateful child!" he spat. "Get out of my sight! Go!" And he shot forwards, inducing her to flinch, before slapping her hard across the face.

Hand covering her throbbing cheek, Isla tore up to her room, yanking the door behind her, and grabbing her phone, dialled Jen's number.

"Jen, he's gone mad, screaming at me," she sobbed. *"He hit me too. Can you come round? I'm scared."*

"Don't worry, sweetheart," she reassured. *"I'm on my way."*

"Thanks, Jen."

"Take deep breaths, stay in your room and lock the door."

"I will, but please hurry." And she put the latch down, hid under the thick covers and waited, cheek smarting and heart pounding fiercely.

A while later, the bell rang and rang, until she heard cursing and footsteps.

"What the hell – *you*!" he yelled, on opening. "You have the audacity to come here! Are you mad!"

"Oh no, on the contrary, very sane indeed, thank you," Jen replied composedly, using the opportunity to put her foot in the door and edge forwards. "I've come to talk to you, that's all. And judging from your tone, I assume you already know that Ava has left the sanatorium. I'd just like a civil dialogue, with no shouting, so that we may go over recent events in a composed manner, allowing me time to clarify anything which requires elucidation."

The tone of Jen's voice had seemed to assuage him slightly and he strode ahead of her into the lounge.

"Firstly," she stated, following him into the room and sitting down, "I'd like to make it abundantly clear that the latest developments had nothing whatsoever to do with Isla. On hearing of my friend's predicament, I merely wanted to help, and I think we're agreed that we are on the same page here," she continued diplomatically, knowing categorically that he wasn't.

Peter bristled, and huffed, but surprisingly said nothing.

"You must realise that you can't keep Isla from her mother. She was so distressed that she came to find me and explained the wretched situation Ava was in. I'm sure you can see that being prescribed copious amounts of drugs every day is not conducive to a quick recovery; this treatment was not helping her at all. I contacted Abbie and we decided that taking Ava back to Cornwall for a while would be the best medicine; and when she feels better, she will, naturally, come back home." A move she hoped Ava would not make any time soon. "I know we are all concerned about Ava's welfare," she continued steadily. "And we all want the best for her."

There was silence, before Peter shuffled in his chair and looked up.

"You should have kept your nose out of our business. Isla's fine and I don't want Ava crying and moping about, disturbing everyone's peace. She's crazy at the moment and the sanatorium is the best place – and I'm in charge of my wife, not you!" he replied, now raising his voice.

"Well, I have to disagree with your stipulations on two counts: firstly, Isla is not happy without her mother; I know because she told me. Secondly, the fresh sea air and Abbie's love is, at present, the best tonic for Ava and will make her well again."

How she had managed to remain unruffled talking to this vile man, she had no inkling; but now, she realised it was time to go, just in case his temper would resurface.

"Anyway, I'll leave you in peace now. I just wanted to explain. We would, of course, have kept you averse of developments, but knew your work schedule recently has been particularly time-consuming."

"Have you quite finished? 'Cause I'd like you out of my house right now. You're a prying bitch, and I don't appreciate you sticking your nose in. Are we clear?"

"Crystal." And she marched to the front door and let herself out.

Once safely inside her car, she let loose a multitude of expletives, which issued forth like angry gunshots. And not until a modicum of calm had eased her rage, did she text Isla.

Do you want me to stay for a bit? she offered. *I'm outside in the car.*

Um… No, it should be OK now. At least he knows and that's a huge relief. Thanks, Jen – for helping. Means a lot.

That's fine, sweetheart. I'm here whenever you need me.

Could I come to the café tomorrow? Maybe bring Emily?

Of course! You don't need to ask. But try and get some sleep now.

I'll try.

Good. See you soon. Night.

Night.

Just a few minutes later, however, Peter's thunderous voice struck the landing, causing Isla to tremble involuntarily.

"Isla, get downstairs!" he bellowed.

"Coming," she said, hurriedly throwing on her dressing gown and taking the stairs two at a time.

"I'm warning you," he threatened, striding out of the lounge and into the hall to meet her. "Keep away from that woman; she's never been anything but trouble! Do you hear me?"

Isla stood stock-still and said nothing.

"Well, do you?!" he bawled.

She gave a vague nod.

"Right, good. Now get to bed," he ordered. "I've had just about enough for one day. I'm off to the pub."

And as he hadn't come home by morning, Isla deduced he'd either passed out on a bench somewhere or gone back to someone's house – probably a woman's. So, relieved indeed to have breakfasted alone, she left a note saying she'd be working in the library after school, then fed Marmalade, packed a lunch, slung her school bag over her shoulder and headed for the bus stop.

Sweet Retreat

Despite freezing to death in the ill-insulated classroom (her predicament not helped by having forgotten her sweatshirt), Isla's immersion in the lesson had been so intense that she was almost sad when the bell rang.

"It's amazing, this book, isn't it?" she enthused to Emily as they spilled into the corridor.

"*Of Mice and Men*, you mean?" her friend replied absently while checking her messages.

"Duh! Yes, of course. Keep up."

"What? Oh, yeah," she replied, concentrating now. "I feel sorry for poor Lennie, he's one of the few kind characters in it. You just want to hug him."

"Oh God, I wouldn't go that far!" Isla shuddered. "Look what happened to Curley's wife! I bet she wishes she hadn't asked him to stroke her hair!"

"He didn't mean to hurt her though, bless him."

"I know, *but* – poor woman," declared Isla, before adding, "what about Curley? He's vile, isn't he!"

"*So* vile," came Emily's reply.

"In fact, my dad's a bit like Curley," mused Isla. "A tall version, that is – but without the glove filled with Vaseline!" She laughed. "Ugh!"

"Soo gross!" said her friend, wincing. "Who would even do that?" And, giggling, they put two fingers to their mouths and retched. "He treats his wife like a piece of meat," continued Emily, her face suddenly serious. "Why does she put up with it? I don't get it."

"It's sad... and complicated." Isla sighed. "I guess she thinks there are no other options. Hey, listen," she said, changing the subject. "I'm going to see my mum's friend, Jen, after school, she owns a café in Camden. Do you want to come with me?"

"Um, yes OK, sounds good. I'll ask Mum to make sure, but it should be fine."

"She makes awesome cakes."

"Right, in that case, I'm definitely coming! I'll text you later."

And the friends drifted into their next lesson.

At the end of the school day, Isla checked her mobile in eager anticipation, and was delighted to see that Emily could accompany her to the café. As a matter of fact, Isla had dropped by several times since she had confided in Jen, simply informing her father (just in case he noticed her lateness) that an after-school study class had recently been launched in the library. And, not prone to bothering about her whereabouts anyway, he seemed perfectly disposed to believe her little lie.

"I'm glad your mum was OK with us going to Jen's," said Isla.

"Yeah, it's all good; she just wants to know *everything* I do, which is a bit stifling at times. What about yours?"

"Um... my mum's not very well at the moment, so

she's staying in Cornwall with my granny. I told my father I was revising at the library – that a study group had been organised by the head – cause he's forbidden me to see Jen; he hates her."

"Wow, harsh!" replied Emily, raising her eyebrows. "Yes, sometimes a white lie's far easier. What's wrong with your mum?"

"She has a broken heart."

Emily met Isla's glance, before asking, "Aren't your parents together anymore then?"

There was a pause before Isla responded.

"I do hope not; but, at the end of the day, who knows?" And they left it at that.

"So, tell me about the cakes!" said Emily. "I'm famished. Does your mum's friend have pastries?"

"Jen. Oh yes, and they're all light and buttery. She makes them herself; there's a fresh supply each day."

"Awesome, can't wait – I'm literally drooling."

"Yuck! That word *drooling*! Reminds me of that vile kid – what's his name again?"

"Dom, as you well know! Dom the pervert. He stares at everyone's tits and it's like he's waiting for lunch the way he salivates."

"Anna is *actually* going out with him now! She must be crazy!"

"Yes, or desperate! Do you think they've *done it*?"

"Ugh! I hope not. Just imagine him slobbering, like a spittle-spraying camel, all over her private bits. Slurpy, slurp!"

And they roared so much that Isla's sides hurt, and she genuinely thought she might wet herself.

She felt so relaxed with Emily; they joked constantly on the bus, laughing out loud, so much so that an elderly woman delivered a disparaging frown, causing them to erupt into further hyenic giggles, albethey muffled this time.

It was so good just being a teenager again! And Isla basked in her current happiness.

Home by the Sea

Poor Ava, she had become so thin – skeletal, in fact – and Abbie's heart broke. How could such torment have gone on for all this time without her knowledge? She fought back a tear. Thank God Isla had had the foresight to alert Jen. Thank God!

Ava slept a lot on their return, and for the first few days her mother had allowed it, just popping in every now and again with a glass of water or bowl of soup. After this initial respite, however, she deemed it time for her daughter to venture out onto the patio to recline in the cosy, cushioned rocking chair.

At first the fragile girl just sat, languidly gazing at the papery red poppies and dots of tiny birds pecking at the velvet-green grass. But gradually, a sprinkling of watery words trickled forth, spilling into streamlets, which, drop by drop, rose to rills of revelation; and riding on a firm wave of veracity, her hitherto captive story was duly unleashed… and Abbie listened as Ava's heart-rending tale shattered the stillness.

"I can't exactly remember when things started to go wrong," she mused. "I know he disliked Jen from the start, he made that abundantly clear, and she saw it immediately. He was jealous of our friendship, that's for sure. And that was constantly a problem, which grew despite my efforts to appease him. In the end, he forbade me to see her at all, and I was scared that if I did, he would…"

"Would what, sweetheart?" asked Abbie tentatively.

"Um…" And she hesitated.

"It's OK, you can tell me."

"Well, when he found out we'd been in touch, I could see the fury in his eyes, but Isla was there, so he left for the pub. Later that evening, though, when she was in bed, he attacked me – slapped my face, gripped my arms, and spat out the word: *Bitch!* Over and over. My face throbbed, my arms were bruised and painful, but worse, my spirit was crushed. And… um… over the years he'd pushed me into this dark space, until I became a mere shadow, gradually cut off from all my friends – just like Jen had predicted. I was left completely alone. *Why the hell didn't I listen to her?*" And she put her head in her hands before continuing. "I simply seemed to accept him putting me down as if it were normal. I even thought it was my fault that he got angry. *How could I have been so stupid?*"

"It's more complicated than that," mused Abbie. "The important thing is that you are actually talking about it."

That night, Abbie was woken by screaming and, on rushing into her daughter's room, observed Ava, beads of sweat glistening on her face, crying out: *"No, no, don't take her. I won't let you. Please…."*

"Darling, shh, shh," she soothed. "Just a bad dream. You're safe now. Go back to sleep."

"I'm so useless. I shouldn't have said those things about Peter, should I? I feel so guilty. Maybe they're not true at all and I made it all up. Maybe he's right, it's my over-active imagination again. Why am I scared all the time? Of everything! I've made such a mess of my life!"

"That's not true. Of course you haven't. It's just draining talking about all this. You've bottled up so much over the years, to finally find your voice again, and talk, it's very brave and I admire you. It is a huge step forward, and you shouldn't feel guilty – for anything. Believe me, Ava, you are not to blame."

Relaxing in her mother's arms, Ava nodded weakly, before shutting her weary eyes. And Abbie held her close, singing sotto voce until she slept. *We'll take it day by day*, she mused inwardly. *It's going to be a long journey. I just thank God we've made a start.*

"Poor Isla," sighed Ava the following afternoon. "It's so difficult for her, and it's my fault. I let her down."

"No, you didn't, darling. You did the very best you could, given the circumstances."

"I'd have been such a brilliant mother, if only I'd left him."

"Ah yes, the futile *if onlys* where life would have been sugar-coated and candyfloss-cushioned." And Abbie smiled. "Please don't beat yourself up. You are a good mother. Isla doesn't judge you; she loves you. She was the one who contacted Jen and got us all to help get you away from that awful place."

"I know," came the faint response. "But why did I let all of this happen? And if Isla *is* disappointed in me, who could blame her? So often I was on antidepressants and sleeping tablets that I doddered round in a permanent daze. I didn't play with her, or even talk to her, *I couldn't*, I felt numb the whole time. And if I stopped taking them, which I did on occasion, I was consumed by anxiety and irritation and would snap at her for no reason at all."

"Now, don't you talk like that. Believe me when I say that Isla does not blame you; she's on your side, that's very clear, and she wants you to get better with all her heart."

"Mum, I've missed her so much. You have no idea."

"Darling, I do; of course I do. But now you need rest. Cast all thoughts aside. I'll fetch you some hot milk and honey and we'll talk more tomorrow. OK?"

"Yes, and thanks. I love you so much."

"I love you too. It'll be OK, we'll get this sorted. Be patient, give it time."

And a faded smile dusted over Ava's lips.

The next morning, on venturing downstairs, Abbie was surprised to see Ava sitting at the kitchen table, head in a book, with a cup of freshly made coffee perched on a mat in front of her.

"Oh, how nice to see you up already," she said. "What are you reading?"

"*Franny and Zooey.* I found it on your bookshelf." Ava paused, before adding, "Listen to this: *Why are you breaking down incidentally? I mean if you're able to go into a collapse with all your might, why can't you use the same energy to stay well and busy?* It all seems so obvious. So why can't I do that?"

"Don't worry, darling, you'll get there. And you're already on your way – you should be proud. It's ages since I read that book, but if I remember correctly, Franny finds peace in the end, and so will you."

Later that afternoon, Ava stared up at the clear blue sky. "It's beautiful," she sighed. "But it's like I'm looking in from a distance, as if I'm separate somehow, an observer. Yet the beauty still seems so stark and renders me devoid of energy. Does any of this make sense?" And she turned to Abbie expectantly, as if her answers would contain a valley full of wisdom to soothe her disquietude.

Deeming it fit, however, to offer only a few words, Abbie replied, "What you say makes *perfect* sense, darling. But for now, just *know* that things will change; you really won't stay like this for ever, believe me."

And mother and daughter sat quietly, the warmth of the sun gently comforting, soothing, healing.

But sadly, it was not long before the familiar torment had returned, cruelly wiping out Ava's prior peace. And now her words erupted into the still air, worrying small birds in the bushes, and causing squirrels to abandon the nuts Abbie had kindly put out for them, in favour of scurrying up the nearest tree.

"I can't think straight anymore, thoughts of *him* keep haunting me!"

"Then talk," coaxed Abbie patiently. "Get it out of your system."

"You must be so sick of my whining," she said, chewing her lower lip.

"On the contrary, sweetheart. I want to help, so tell me – tell me all."

And Ava spoke, her words rushing for release.

"He got into my head – all the time… made me feel I was worthless, incapable of completing even basic tasks, from cooking simple dishes, to washing up, to… oh God, I don't know – *everything!* But the *very worst* was when he quietly criticised the way I was with Isla. He'd whisper things in my ear – unpleasant things, contradicting me, telling me I was talking rubbish, that I shouldn't have said what I did; sometimes outwardly refuting my words in front of her – just quietly injecting venom into the already gaping wound. A snake-like predator, that's what he was. At first, I'd protest, but that would cause him to shout, so in the end I'd remain still, unable to move – useless, like a toy without its batteries."

"Oh, my poor darling. What you must have gone through." And Abbie held her daughter's hand, careful to mask her growing concern.

"Do you think he'll turn up here and force me to go back?" asked Ava, the following morning, panic surfacing in her voice. "And what about Isla? Is she OK, on her own with him? What have I done?"

"No, it's what *he* has done. Listen to me, Isla would *know* if he decided to come here and she would ring, so don't waste time thinking about that. And she's fine. Trust me. She speaks to you every day. She's a strong young woman and is perfectly capable of looking after herself."

"Because of me, she's had to," lamented Ava.

"Look, she's OK, so please stop with all this guilt. Fetch your jacket; we're going for a long walk and after that we'll drop in at The Anchor Inn for a beer and pub lunch."

"Oh, I'm not sure…"

"Yes, you are. Hurry up."

"Fine, you win," Ava conceded, resignedly unhooking her jacket. And, like a small child, she trailed behind her mother, out of the house and into the beckoning sunshine.

Vicious Vibes

Pam could scarcely suppress her wry smirk as Peter stormed, like a wild bull, into her living room the next afternoon.

"Ava's gone!" he spat, pouring himself a glass of brandy. "She left the asylum and went with her mother to Cornwall! *How bloody dare she*? And Isla knew all about it. She was *there* with that odious cow, Jen! I'll not have it! Ava's gone too far this time; she'll pay for this."

"Do compose yourself!" piped Pam, perched erect on a teak dining chair. "My advice is this: leave her, Peter! She'll be off your hands; you don't want her now, anyway, do you? After all the trouble she's been."

"But – that's not the point." He swept his hand roughly through his now-tousled hair. "She's disappeared without my permission, and she's supposed to be my wife! I won't have it; I'm driving to Cornwall to get her back! I'll make her sorry she caused me this inconvenience."

"Look, Peter, think carefully. She's not what you deserve. Just divorce the pathetic woman! She didn't give you the son you wished for, and she ended up in a mad house – the *shame* of it! So what's the use of her? Tell me that. You've got plenty of other women at your beck and call."

He paused, taking in her resolute words, before saying, "But what about Isla?"

"I've told you enough times, Isla is a big disappointment, and you know it – and that's her mother's fault. Just get them both out of your life and move on."

Pam was in complete control. Her hard heart beat at a steady pace; the blood pulsed powerfully through the vein on her neck, and an imperiously defiant drive lit up her dull, taut face until it shone like a beacon.

"Alright," he concorded. "I'll let it go for now. I need to think."

"Good, that's settled then; I'll prepare some food." And despite herself, she revealed a rare smile as she proceeded purposefully to the kitchen. Soon she would have her nephew to herself again. Soon those intruders would be out of their lives – forever.

Twelfth Night

"Hi, Ems. God, you look like a total Goth; what's that all about? Is that your mum's wedding dress?"

"Actually, at the beginning of the play, I'm supposed to be grieving, so I made my face pale and my eyes dark, from all Olivia's crying. And, in Shakespeare's time, *duh*, people wore white for mourning, unless I just made that up. Anyhow, it's my interpretation, so deal with it!" And she pulled a comic face.

"OK, OK, I totally get it now," grinned Isla. "And you look divine!"

"Thanks."

"Oh God, I wonder what Sir Toby will wear – how the hell did we get lumbered with Dirty Dom in our group? Thankfully, though, he'll be doing most of his slavering into a tankard – or snogging Anna. Good job she volunteered to play Maria! In fact, she was the only one who did. Surprise, surprise. But most important is we're all safe from any lecherous advances on stage. Phew!" And she mopped her brow dramatically.

"Thank the lord for that! Hey, where's your costume, Feste?"

"You seriously think I'm coming to school *on the bus* in a jester's costume? Pray, think again! I'll change during break."

"'K, fine. I'm wearing mine cause I like the attention," chuckled Emily, swishing dramatically into her first lesson.

A while later, as Isla self-consciously jingled her way into the drama studio, tight chausses clinging like ivy to her slim legs and jester's cap alive with hanging bells, like partying nits, her attempts to appear serene and unflustered went entirely out of the window. *Where was Emily?* She'd feel infinitely better if her friend were near. Why was she so apprehensive? Emily would be cool, confident, and this seemingly effortless ease, without fail, always rubbed off on her.

However, when, on tentatively glancing round, she glimpsed Dom in the corner – awkwardly gripping a pewter tankard perched precariously on a belly puffed up like popcorn, courtesy of a huge cushion inserted into his oversized doublet, which, in turn, bulged out over limp, baggy trunk hose – a nervous giggle issued from her lips, allowing her to relax a bit. And observing his wretchedly embarrassed face semi-hidden behind a dark wig of straggly long hair, she knew that at least there was one person who appeared more ridiculous than her!

Shortly, the teacher rushed into the studio, nervous enthusiasm and anticipation further colouring her already ruddy features.

"Wow!" she cried, trying too hard to be jolly. "Well

done, all of you. You've made such a grand effort. Now listen carefully. Try to ignore the examiners, and if you can't, imagine them stark naked and you'll feel better."

The class erupted into a sea of overzealous giggles.

"OK, OK – wind down, they'll be here any minute. Deep breaths and *break a leg*."

"We couldn't do the play then, Miss," giggled Daniel.

"Oh, *please*. Not now, *dumb arse*," muttered Isla under her breath, her irritation borne largely, but not wholly, out of stress.

"*Isla!*" chastised Emily, feigning shock as she appeared behind her. "You're so mean! Daniel's harmless enough; stupid, I'll grant you, but benign."

"Ems, there you are!" she replied, ignoring her friend's riposte altogether.

"Yes, here I am. So, what's up? Come on, spit it out."

"I'm so scared," confessed Isla helplessly. "What if I mess up? I can't even remember my lines! My mind's gone blank."

"*You? Scared?* Come on, you'll be totally fine. And if you need prompting, Daniel will be behind the screen when we're on stage." She smiled, struggling to mask her doubt with reassurance.

"And that's supposed to make me feel better *how*?" complained Isla, trying, unsuccessfully, to steady her shaking hands.

"Don't worry, you won't need him anyway; we've gone over your part so many times, you could deliver the words backwards. Just take a deep breath and, like Miss said, think of all the examiners naked – with their tiny peckers, shrivelled balls, and frizzy pussies," she whispered wickedly under her breath. And the pair's giggles could scarcely be contained, despite both hands tightly pressing against quivering lips, as they shared this private joke until they were fit to burst.

"Come on, everyone! Take your positions," projected the teacher with deafening positivism. "And don't forget to ace the Shakespearean language; it's important to demonstrate a clear understanding of textual detail. Lots of expression! Project! Don't be nervous. Enjoy yourselves! All good."

"Not gonna lie, she seems a tad edgy *herself*." Isla giggled as they scuttled, like excitable mice, behind the heavy drapes to await their imminent fate.

The weary-looking examiners, struggling to feign even a modicum of fervour, were speedily ushered to their seats as the teacher, providing a complete contrast with her semi-hysterical zeal, dealt pleasantries regarding the weather, desired snacks, if they required a bottle of water, more desk space… the list went on. And once all was in order and the team settled, she hurriedly hopped up the stairs, almost tripping over her shoelace, which had, unnoticed, gradually come undone, before whizzing backstage and whispering emphatically, "Right, ready. Give it your best."

And, within seconds, there was Daniel bouncing onto the stage dressed as Viola in lacy dress, silk tights and shiny shoes, rouge smothered a tad too generously over each cheek.

"Looks like a clown," muttered Isla quietly from behind the curtain.

"You've got it in for him, haven't you!" Emily held her

hand firmly. "Chill, it'll be fine. And if you remember, *you're* the clown!"

And, despite resistance, a fleck of amusement touched Isla's lips.

"Welcome, all," he bellowed self-consciously. "I'd like to introduce our selected scenes from *Twelfth Night* by William Shakespeare. We hope you enjoy our performance." And introduction duly delivered, he launched into an animated enactment of Viola's fraught arrival in Illyria, before scrambling to the safety of backstage, very nearly knocking Isla over in the process.

"*Watch it,*" she snarled.

"Ha-ha, revenge is sweet," whispered Emily. "OK, we good to go?"

"As good as we'll ever be. Break a leg."

"You too."

The performance was a triumph! Avid clapping ensued from the audience, the examiners appearing far happier than when they came in. And as the entire cast bowed repeatedly, a sense of elation wrapped around them like a veritable royal robe.

Indeed, Isla was in her element: the role of Feste suited her to perfection. Witty wordplay fuelled her fervour, and singing love songs *tongue-in-cheek* was definitely her forte. Observing the examiners smiling egged her on to rise to a stellar performance – indeed, the best thus far; and she didn't even have to imagine them naked!

Emily, too, excelled in her role as Olivia and relished the sharp, snappy dialogue with Feste all the more due to Isla's vigour and verve; they bounced off each other effortlessly. And Dom nailed his part as Sir Toby Belch, delighting in the constant belching required of the character – as suggested by the name – and canoodled zealously, like a slobbering bulldog, with Maria, played admirably by Anna, who blushed until her face was beetroot.

Daniel's depiction of Viola in the shipwreck scene, heavy with hyperbole, had him wildly clawing the sand as he crawled to shore; and he delivered more than adequately when Viola disguised herself as her twin brother, Cesario – except that he forgot to change his shoes, but that didn't matter one iota.

"Told you all would be fine," enthused Emily.

"And, as usual, you were right," nodded Isla, her jester's hat jingling in jolly accordance.

Momentary Dilemma

The gnarled-up sensation in Peter's head was constant, every day interfering with his peace of mind. He felt powerless, emasculated, and he wanted to kill someone. This churned-up anger rarely left him, and drinking, which he did frequently, usually fuelled it.

Aunt Pam had advised him to let Ava go – Isla too – but a hot fury roused him, reminding him of his childhood and absent parents, who, perpetually working or partying – at least, that's what his aunt had said; he couldn't really remember – had made him feel invisible. Pam had stepped in, even when they were alive, and taken him under her wing. He couldn't go against her, yet somehow, he knew he had to follow this through. He had to punish Ava.

Isla didn't really feature in his concerns; she was simply there, living in his house. He supposed, with a mere nanosecond of regret, that, regarding his neglect of her, he was no better than his parents in many respects. And, just like when he was a child, his shoulders ached. But she seemed happy enough, he reassured himself.

And Ava. *Had he ever loved her?* At first, maybe, but he wanted her to do everything his way, and she was so very difficult, with a mind of her own; too independent, yes, that was it. He needed to have power over her, to dominate; and, at the start she protested, but gradually, once he'd forced her to yield, he felt formidable. He was no longer a timid child, but a man! How dare Ava try to escape him!

Later, he would explain everything to Pam. He needed her to understand. But Isla must not know; she could not be trusted. And so the decision was made. He would drive down to Cornwall at the weekend and sort Ava out!

Picnic on the Beach

Abbie decided that a picnic in the fresh air would hopefully lift Ava's spirits, so she prepared some of her daughter's favourite foods in an attempt to encourage her to eat more, as her face was gaunt, which was a worry for her mother.

"I don't really feel up to going out, Mum," she groaned as Abbie breezed into her room and drew back the curtains.

"Nonsense. You're not going to languish in bed for another day. A day out will do you good, put some colour in your cheeks. Have a shower and I'll prepare poached eggs on toast for you."

"Thanks, Mum, but I'm not hungry."

"You need to eat something, darling, and this will be a very light option."

"OK, I guess so." And robotically, Ava dragged her tired body to the shower.

The sun, like a Seville orange, lit up the sky as Abbie lay down the picnic rug.

"Now, what more encouragement can you need

before I see a smile?" But she knew, in her heart, it would take oh so much more than this.

Ava blinked as she gazed up at the bright, burning ball of unfailing certainty, confidence, presence. *Would she ever feel happy again?* she wondered sadly, lowering her fragile frame onto the blue, checked rug.

They stretched out, embraced by the warm blanket of sunshine, and Abbie held her daughter's hand. No words were spoken. Only the warmth, and the constancy of the sea, soothed and lulled her into a sublime state of calm she had not enjoyed since before she had met Peter.

A few hours later, Abbie opened the picnic hamper, tempting Ava with a wealth of gastronomical fare: delightful, matured cheeses, cold meats, sweet, ripe figs with torn-basil and lemon. And Ava tentatively tasted a starling's portion washed down with a small glass of juice.

It was later that she felt ready to say more, and Abbie listened quietly.

"Do you think I'm pathetic, Mum? A liability?"

"Good gracious, of course not, darling. You're extremely brave to have endured such toxic behaviour. How could you possibly think otherwise?"

And Ava hugged her mother before continuing.

"It was awful, Mum. When Isla was born, he was jealous of the attention she received; his belligerence grew, and he forever insisted I spend more time with him and him alone. I explained that there were three of us now, but he showed precious little interest in Isla; he definitely saw her as a threat to the prior exclusivity of our relationship. It was as if he felt he were relinquishing control now that another person had my love. And during that period, he nearly lost his first job: he was disciplined for *displaying overly aggressive comportment* towards workmates, which was especially highlighted on a team-building trip, where he had been adamant his proposals were the only ones worthy of consideration. He refused unequivocally to listen to colleagues' views, until, at one point, he actually punched someone.

"Things got worse then. He took his frustrations out on me, often putting me down in front of Isla. He said I was useless; and every single day, my confidence was shaken, until I became a stranger to my former self.

"It was then that I decided I'd like to join a local Pilates group; the fitness centre was close to home, so travelling time would be at a minimum. I hoped a new interest would enable me to meet people and this might raise my spirits. But when I broached the subject, he dismissed my idea instantly, declaring that I should be at home with him, that I didn't care about Isla – *"and who the hell is going to look after her. It's your bloody job!"* he'd said. It was just once a week, that's all – for a mere hour. But I couldn't go against him because I was scared. Mum, can we just go home?" said Ava, patting her sore eyes with a tissue.

"I've got a better idea. Take your shoes off; we're going for a paddle."

Driving to Cornwall

"You bloody stupid imbecile!" stormed Peter (already self-recriminating for not obeying Pam) when a driver, grimacing in angry frustration, flashed him repeatedly, in a vain attempt to halt his reckless gunning down the M4. This wholly justifiable action, unsurprisingly, stirred Peter yet further until his face resembled a belligerent bull, and on the instant, he veered, this madman, into the fast lane, amassing a speed of 130 miles per hour in the now relatively seasoned Porsche he had bought in more lucrative days.

"Ava, you scheming bitch! It's your fault I'm here. Your fault I went against Pam! I'll get you for this and you'll be sorry, believe me!" And the words were spat out like venom.

*

Snuggled up under the duvet, book in hand, Isla stroked Marmalade, his eyes smiling slits of rapture. Indeed, it was not until 11.30am that she surfaced, showered, and made her way to the kitchen for breakfast.

And there resting on the table, propped up against the salt pot, leant a brief note – brevity regarding communication being her father's signature. And she sighed before pulling it towards her.

Gone to Pam's.

And as he spent a considerable amount of time at Pam's, she was not remotely suspicious.

*

By the time Isla finds out, it will be too late! Too late to warn Ava and that interfering witch, Jen! And a satisfied sneer crept over his tight lips, as he accelerated with an almost sexual fervour, ripping past the line of cars, which shone steel-like in the gleaming sun.

Lightbulb Moment

After successfully completing an essay on *Of Mice and Men*, beyond doubt one of her favourite school texts thus far, Isla decided a lunch in Sweet Retreat was merited; and she hoped Jen might have time for a chat, even though Saturdays, she realised, were always the busiest. In truth, she missed her mother; they had video chats most days, but this was, naturally, not the same as being with her.

Wistfully she ventured into the hall to grab her coat and bag, but with an abrupt jolt, stood stock-still, having suddenly noticed the absence of her father's holdall bag – normally perched, fully packed, against the wall, due to his constant trips. He never took it to Pam's, so something was definitely amiss.

Panic sent a rush of blood coursing through her, causing her heart to drum wildly, and briskly tearing open the zip of her rucksack, she grabbed her secret phone. But although Jen's number should be fixed in her memory, fear crippled her. *Which way round were the digits? Contacts. Contacts. Where were they?*

Eventually finding Sweet Retreat on Google, she pressed the phone icon.

"*Hello? This is Sweet Retreat. How may I help you?*" came a relaxed voice.

"*Is Jen there?*" she asked, striving to mask her rising angst.

"*She's in the kitchen, baking. Give me your number and I'll ask her to ring back when she's finished. Who's calling?*"

"*It's Isla. Listen, this is a matter of urgency. I need to speak to her straight away.*"

"*Oh hi, Isla. Don't worry, I'll get her right now – bear with.*"

The seconds that passed before Jen came to the phone were an eternity to Isla, and butterflies flapped wildly against the wall of her stomach.

"*Hi, Isla, it's Jen. What's the matter?*"

And the child gasped in relief before explaining her dilemma in a frenzied tone.

"*Jen, his bag is gone. He left a note saying he was visiting Pam, but he never takes it to hers, he's got stuff there already, so I think he wanted to put me off the scent. I'm pretty sure he's driving down to Cornwall.*"

There was a pause as Jen endeavoured to process this new information.

"*Are you still there?*" enquired Isla, a tight, clam-like knot gripping her gut.

"*Yes, I'm here. Now listen to me. First, you need to phone Ava and warn her, although if he left early, he could well have arrived already. I'll find someone to cover for me, nip home to collect a few things, fill up with petrol and come straight to you. Don't worry, just pack some clothes and toiletries.*"

"*What about Marmalade?*" she asked quietly.

"*Unless you know anyone who can look after him at short notice…?*"

"*No. I'll bring him; he's got a pet carrier.*"

"*And remember to lock doors, switch off lights. All good. See you soon, sweetheart. We got this.*"

Without delay, Isla rang her mother's number, but there was no answer, then Abbie's, but to no avail. *Oh my God, what's happened?* she mouthed frantically. *Where are you? Pick up!*

Next, she tried the landline. *Nothing!* What in heaven's name should she do now?

Suddenly, however, came the realisation that Jen would be over soon, expecting her to be ready. So, after swiftly bounding upstairs to fling a few random items of clothing into her rucksack, she plucked up the blissfully dozing cat, now in a surly state of vexation at having been disturbed, before hastening down the stairs to retrieve the pet carrier from the corner of the conservatory.

A bemused look on his face, Marmalade allowed himself, contrary to the norm, to be placed inside without a struggle. Maybe, sensing Isla's acute agitation, he discerned a certain gravity concerning their new predicament and decided it would be wise to comply.

Impending Danger

Darting through narrow, winding roads, which, oblivious of any threat, shepherded the way, like thin ribbons, to his final destination, Peter snarled; his only recently curbed anger returning as he recalled, due to a mini roundabout adorned with painted pebbles, his proximity to Abbie's cottage.

"Not long now, Ava. What a surprise you're in for; you have no idea!"

*

"There was no answer when I called Mum," bemoaned Isla, slamming the front door and following Jen to the car. "What can we do?"

"Not a lot, I'm afraid, sweetheart," replied Jen resignedly. "We just need to make a move and think positively. I know it's hard but try not to worry."

Isla nodded before tossing her rucksack randomly into the boot and, hurriedly positioning the carrier on the back seat directly facing her, so that Marmalade wouldn't be subjected to any more stress than absolutely necessary, she lowered herself onto the padded seat. Soon after, her tired eyes closed, allowing her to drift into a surprisingly sound sleep, given the daunting circumstances. Her repose was well-timed, considering the sea of mobile metal now surrounding them.

Indeed, all the vehicles in the entire country must be travelling down to Cornwall, mused Jen resignedly as she loosened her grip on the steering wheel, which, under the glaring eyes of the afternoon sun and the sweaty grasp of her overheated hands, had become damp and slippery.

Half an hour later, a mere litre of now-warm water remained, and the traffic was at a complete standstill. Frustration had Jen clenching her fists before reaching for her phone in an anguished attempt to get through to Ava. No response. *Was he already there?* And a steely dread seized her. *Were they too late? Would Ava be on her way back to London by now? And where, in heaven's name, was Abbie?* Something was awry, and a visceral shiver passed through her like a ghost.

Back Home

After deadheading some geraniums, Abbie unlocked the front door and led the way into the hallway.

"Thanks, Mum. Today has done me a power of good. My whole body feels less tense. I might even go swimming tomorrow."

"Excellent idea," replied Abbie, delighted to see her daughter more at ease.

"I'd like to phone Isla for a video chat, but it has to be after seven when she's in her room, with no chance of Peter being near," Ava continued as she reached into her beach-bag for her mobile.

"Then let's have a glass of wine first, while the sun's still out," suggested Abbie.

"Good idea. I'll put my phone on charge and join you right away."

And the two women strolled contentedly into the garden, gently lowering themselves onto the blue-cushioned deckchairs which overlooked the trickling fountain issuing from the crown of some exquisite Greek goddess fashioned in marble, and they soaked up the peace of late afternoon while sipping chilled wine.

What a perfect day it had been. Just perfect.

So engrossed in conversation were they, that the sound of a car crawling almost silently, like a predator, along the far end of the drive did not, at first, reach their ears. Indeed, it was not until Ava inadvertently turned her head, to follow the sweeping path of a flight of swallows, that she saw him, standing solidly in the centre of the path, blocking out the sun, his eyes cold as flint. Her body froze in disbelief as the prior halcyon moment was stolen, stamped on in an instant, and, eyes wide, she exuded a rasping gasp, inducing Abbie to jolt and instantly follow her gaze.

"Well, well, well," came the scathing tone she was so familiar with, which made her skin prickle. "So here you are, Ava. Hiding with your mother. And what a merry dance you've led me. Running away. *Run rabbit run.* But I'm here now. Here to take you home, home to your husband – that's me, Ava. Oh, and your only child… remember Isla? I must say she's not impressed with your behaviour either and deeply regrets being forced to go to the sanatorium to witness your foolhardy ruse."

Ava knew this to be untrue. He had no inkling of the existence of Isla's mobile, not the slightest idea that they talked most days. Not a clue. And the faintest of smiles tentatively allowed itself to cross her pale lips.

"Oh, you think this is amusing, do you?" he hissed, catching her expression. "Letting everyone down – again."

"No, no – of course not, I didn't mean—" came her anxious and mumbled reply.

"I think it's best you go, Peter," intervened Abbie,

masking her fears with a calm yet assertive voice. "Ava is resting, recovering – and is in need of peace and quiet."

"*Resting, recovering*, is she?" he snarled. "Well, she can do that just as effectively at home. Come on, Ava, get in the car. We'll discuss this later."

"I... I... could maybe stay here," she replied in cowed tones, now fully yielding to his wrath.

"No, Ava. I'll not leave until you get in the car. Don't try my patience anymore. Just get in!" And his thin lips formed a tight grey line like taut wire.

"You heard my daughter; she'll be staying here with me," asserted Abbie. "And you should leave. You're not welcome."

"Leave?!" He was shouting now. "Leave, you say? – *without my wife*?! I've driven all the way down here – to *leave*!"

"Yes, but you weren't invited so you've wasted your time," continued Abbie with stern resolve. "And please refrain from raising your voice."

Like a shot, this challenge to his authority punched an ugly defiance, a ghastly grimace, over his face, prompting him to lunge forward with razor-sharp intent, grab Ava's arm, and frog-march her to the car. And when, instinctively, Abbie rushed to intercept him, she was thrust violently to the ground.

"Please, leave my mother alone," cried Ava helplessly. "I'll come with you; just don't hurt her."

With a quiet dignity, Abbie slowly lifted herself to her feet, gently brushing sand and gravel from her shaking legs. And when she spoke, her voice was firm and unwavering.

"Darling, you mustn't go with him. You know why. Peter, let her be. I'll phone the police if you don't leave immediately."

Yet her threats, alas, went unheeded as he bundled Ava roughly onto the passenger seat. The engine fired up without delay and, in a flash of light and celerity, the car disappeared round the corner, leaving Abbie, her eyes glued to the now-empty path, sobbing like a frightened child.

Too Late?

Stirring Abbie from her still-stupefied stance came the shrill sound of her landline. And robotically she pursued the ringing, which transported her into the darkness of the hallway.

"*Hello?*" she muttered, a terrible tiredness shrouding her.

"*Oh, thank God you picked up,*" blurted Jen, her face imbued with relief. "*We've been trying to reach you all day. I need to warn you, Peter's on his way.*"

"*Too late.*" The words were formed with an almost stoical tone, which bothered Jen as it was so unlike Abbie, who usually exuded an intoxicatingly infectious fervour.

"*What's up?*" she uttered, dreading the response.

"*He came earlier. He took Ava.*"

"*Oh God! When did he leave?*"

"*I don't know exactly, but not long since.*"

"*We're too late!*" exclaimed Jen automatically, on reflection adding, "*Listen, will you be OK if we turn around at the next junction? We need to get back to London; that's where he'll be bound for sure.*"

"*Where are you?*"

"On the motorway down to yours. We came as soon as we heard."

"We?"

"Isla's with me."

"I see. Yes, I'll be OK, but, if you go after him, please be careful, won't you. He grabbed Ava and when I tried to stop him, shoved me onto the path."

"What?! Are you hurt?"

"No, I'm fine, but she *needs you. Please tread carefully; he still has power over her – she crumbled completely in his toxic presence."*

"We can turn off at the next junction," stated Jen, her mind solely on imminent action. Thankfully, Isla was still asleep.

"I'll text or call when I can. Try not to worry."

"Ha-ha, a tall order, but yes, I'll try. Will be thinking of you. Good luck." And Abbie placed the receiver on the stand, poured a stiff brandy to calm her nerves, and sank down into the soft folds of the settee.

*

He studied her with growing contempt as the car weaved recklessly in and out of the lanes like a shell-shocked wasp.

"Please keep your eyes on the road, Peter. I'm frightened."

"You're always frightened, Ava. Look at you trembling like a bloody rabbit caught in headlights – pathetic, that's what you are. Take those pills in the glove box; they'll keep you under control."

"But I'm trying to wean myself off them. Where did *you* get them?"

"Never you mind. *Take them, Ava, damn it!*" he seethed, his big hand callously clenching her thin leg, inducing her eyes to water from the pain. "Just swallow the bloody things or you'll cause an accident!"

And, with a gnawing misery, she fumbled around, her hand shaking, until she found the container.

"Take two, Ava, two, OK!"

She obeyed, shuddering at the sharp aftertaste as she washed them down with small sips of bottled water. And then, with glazed eyes, she sat staring blankly at the long road ahead.

*

Wandering aimlessly into Ava's room, Abbie breathed in the still-warm comfort of this safe place: soft linen sheets, pastel-coloured towels, cosy jumper for evenings on the patio… yet all sense of normality had been snatched brutishly away in a matter of minutes. And she had been powerless to stop it. Sadly, she turned to go. However, on noticing a solitary sheet of screwed-up paper peeping out from under the bed, she picked it up and read:

Claws that cruelly scratch and sting,
that pierce and tear,
carve and wound
my paper skin.

Claws that crush my beating heart,
that rip my happy thoughts apart.
Claws that stifle, squeeze and squash.

Claws that burn my soft
pink flesh
to blood-red fire,
lit by a man,
his rage and fury dire.

So let me slip, slide into the cold womb
of a silent sea, where the waves suck and swallow,
until there's no more left of me.

"Oh my dear, darling child!" gasped Abbie. "What has he done to you?"

*

Ava's slight frame occupied a tiny space on the imposing leather seat of Peter's Porsche. She had shrunk far into herself; she wanted to become veiled, vaporous… invisible. The strong medication had already started to cloud her brain. When its process was complete, she would feel blurred, blank… erased. She glanced quietly at his large, solid form and sank even deeper into herself, deeper into nothingness. Funny, the period spent with her mother now seemed like a far-away, distant world – from a long, long time ago. And issuing a feeble sigh, Ava sank into a drug-induced oblivion.

*

"Where are we?" enquired Isla, yawning sleepily from her lengthy repose. "I swear Willow Man should be on the other side of the motorway. Jen, what's happening, we're going in the wrong direction?"

"Yes, something's come up, sweetheart. Peter beat us to it, he's taken Ava; so we're driving back to London. But don't worry, all will be fine, I promise."

"Oh no! He *will* take her straight to the house, won't he?"

"I don't imagine so, not yet anyway; he might think *you're* at home. Pam's would make more sense. But even if he decides to go there, we'll still arrive ahead of him. He must be quite far behind us – I doubt he'll catch up. Anyhow, try not to worry. We got this."

"I hope so." And taking a deep breath, Isla checked on the sleeping cat before gazing vacantly out of the window.

"He used to lock her in the cellar," she muttered after a while. "Sometimes for the whole day."

"Oh, sweetheart, that's awful," replied Jen quietly. "I'm so sorry. Why would he do such a thing?"

"Once, she spilt red wine over a guest during a business lunch; another, he accused her of flirting with a colleague at a company do…" There was a pause. "And, always when he let her out, she'd sit on the sofa and stare into space. I'd tell her about my day when I got home from school and she'd feign interest, but you could tell she was in another place."

"You've been through a lot, haven't you," ventured Jen.

"I used to stroke her hand and fetch her a cup of tea," mused Isla, still staring out of the window.

"That's nice. Often, it's the little things that can make a difference."

"Yeah, I guess so."

Isla released a surprisingly unflustered Marmalade – given his recent upheaval – from the pet carrier and pulled him close, gently caressing his ears until his delighted purring could be heard lightly merging with the sounds of the engine.

They were on their way home – wherever that was.

Arrival in the Capital

Cat's eyes, illumined like a runway, lined the slip road as it hared off the motorway, London-bound. Ava was still dead to the world when Peter's mobile rang. It was Pam.

"Hello, Peter, are you at home?"

"Hi. No, I'm on my way back to London."

"You went to find Ava? When I told you not to."

"Yeah, I know. Sorry. I'll explain later. But I had to get her back. Nobody tricks me like that and gets away with it. And, believe me, she won't do it again."

"So she's with you then?"

"Yes, she's taken some pills, she's sleeping."

"Why don't you come over? I'll make dinner. You can put her in a room at mine if you like – better than going home – but do whatever you think most befitting."

"Thanks, I'll take you up on your offer. Be there in about thirty minutes."

"Fine, I'll put supper on."

It would be good to see Pam; his guilt at not having heeded her prior advice regarding Cornwall bothered him, yet he was certain she'd understand. Also, given he had not eaten since breakfast, he was famished.

As he glanced ahead into an ink-dark sky, dabbed with a smattering of faded stars, his tight lips formed a satisfied smirk, and, ready for a rapid race through the capital, he pressed his foot firmly on the accelerator. He felt calm. So very calm. Now that he had regained control.

On hearing the car door slam, Ava twitched and blinked, like a drowsy dormouse woken early from hibernation. But her befuddled face quickly bore its prior pallor as she registered, with horror, her current predicament. A terrible urge to vomit surfaced as a mere retch, given her empty stomach. Her mouth was parched, but she didn't dare reach for the bottle in the glove box, for fear it would further arouse Peter's fury. Instead, she nestled her soft hands in her small lap and remained silent and still, deeming this the safest stance to adopt, while glancing with guarded discretion via her peripheral vision as Peter's heavy shoes, highlighted by a streetlamp, strode purposefully towards the passenger door, which he flung open, before roughly reaching for her thin arm.

"Right, enough sleep, Ava. Get out, hurry up!" And he yanked her tiny, shivering body out of the car, semi-lifting it, as, like a condemned prisoner, she was frog-marched to the front entrance. Realisation of her whereabouts came all too swiftly, as the stiff, bulky door, with the menacing boom of its brass knocker resounding in her sensitive ears, creaked ajar to reveal the stony gaze of his dreadful aunt. Pam.

*

"We should think about this logically, Isla. We've already established that he won't take Ava home until he's calmed down – just in case you're there – so it's more than likely he'll go to Pam's, which is where you're supposed to think he is anyway. And once he's installed Ava with his awful aunt, he'll return home to check things out, see if you're around, if you know anything."

"But, then what? This is pure conjecture. What comes next?"

"My guess is he'll either try to reinstate Ava in the hospital… *or*… bring her home, where he'll continue to treat her just as he did before she managed to escape his clutches."

Isla sighed in resignation.

"OK," continued Jen. "So, I'll drop you off and then drive to Pam's. That way, we'll cover both possible destinations."

"But I don't want to be at home on my own. *Not now.* And if he *does* come back…"

"I hear you… then what about giving him a ring on the landline? If he answers, you can tell him you're staying the night with Emily and will be back tomorrow. If there's no response, we could pop round, check the house is in darkness, and leave a note on the kitchen table relaying the same message. Then I'll drop you off at my flat and you can stay there. Maybe phone Abbie, that would be a nice idea; let her know we're back."

"Yes, but… oh, never mind, it's just all so very

confusing! Why do I have to come from such a dysfunctional family?"

"Now, now, don't worry. We got this, sweetheart."

"So you keep saying. Well, I hope you're right. I just want my mum back in one piece."

"I know, darling, but mark my words, she'll be fine, just fine."

"Can we go straight back to yours, please? I can't face phoning him or going back to the house."

"Sure, OK," said Jen quietly. "We'll come up with a plan later."

Pam's Confessions

On arrival, Ava's fear may have appeared marginally less acute due to her dazed and dizzy head, yet her edginess and disorientation soon grew to mammoth proportions as Peter dragooned her into the hallway. *Why were they here?* She trembled, a rush of panic flushing through her. *Why hadn't they gone home to see Isla?* There was no escape, she knew that, so she would stay quiet and small, sit where they told her, drink what they gave her, become inanimate, intangible, insensate. And shrouded by her protective sheet, she drifted, like a shadow, into the dining room and sat in the seat indicated by Pam.

"Could you get a glass of water, Pam?" asked Peter, pulling the container full of sleeping pills from his pocket. "Take these, Ava," he ordered, dropping a couple of tablets on the table in front of her. "And go lie on the bed."

Obediently, she held out her hand, dropped the tablets on her tongue, and swept herself into the gloomy, spare room, where she lay, like a pale, porcelain doll, on the cold mattress, gazing at the heavy drapes which forbade any light to enter. After a few minutes, however, on hearing conversation in the other room, she hastily put her hand to her mouth, removed the tablets and placed them soundlessly in a tissue, which she secreted in the lining of the pillow. And, that done, she waited.

It was half an hour before Peter came to check on her, and satisfied she'd be asleep for several hours, he shut the door and returned to the table where dinner was waiting.

"I'm sorry I didn't listen to you, Aunt," he declared between mouthfuls of fillet steak.

Pam sipped her claret steadily before responding. "Peter," she said eventually, "after you'd left, I reconsidered. You were right to bring her back. Think about it. There's a need to be careful. If you let her go, she'll collude with that awful floozie and try to get her mucky paws on your money, your house. Get away with everything! Maybe report you too. We have to employ measures to stop that, at all costs."

"What do you suggest?" he asked, intrigued.

"It's simple. We get rid of her," came the brutally blunt reply.

Having silently nudged the door ajar, in search of an opportunity to escape, Ava, now catching the words *get rid of her*, inadvertently gasped. And, after soundlessly pulling the door to, she darted back to the bed and lay still as death, fearing they may have heard her. Her safety now swayed on a tightrope. It was imperative she find a way out.

"What do you mean *get rid of?*" questioned Peter, agog, a mouthful of runner beans, as yet, undigested.

"What I say. I mean, we make her disappear." And a terrible silence filled the air.

"Disappear? As in, *kill* her?"

"Not so much *kill* as *enable* an accident. Think about it, Peter, it'd be so easy. Drug her, leave her at the top of the stairs – job done; or… submerge her in the bath. It'd be child's play. She has a history of depression; no one would suspect a thing."

"You're joking, aren't you? Or drunk?"

"No, I never joke about things like this. And drunk? Most certainly not." Her chillingly measured voice resounded confidently in the otherwise silent room.

"What about Isla?" he replied, his words taut and discordant.

"Who cares about *her*? You can send her to her grandmother's. She won't cause us any problems." And, with a self-satisfied sigh, she swilled the ruby liquid around her glass. "*Or*… another idea is that we *adjust* the brakes on Ava's car." And a twisted smirk of raw depravity smeared her face as she added: "Like I did with your parents."

Peter gulped. "*What?* What did you say?"

"I *said*, like I did with your parents. I made them disappear you see. I tampered with the brakes, thus causing their fatal accident. It was deserved, I can assure you. They didn't care about *you*… too engrossed in shady business deals, hedonistic lifestyle, immoral parties. I hated your mother!" she raged. "My whole life she was favoured over me – apple of my father's eye – could do no wrong – *whereas me*! I took so many beatings because of her accusations; she made my life miserable.

When you were born, *I* was the one who looked after you. Always. She wasn't the slightest bit interested. *They* weren't interested; but *I* loved you, Peter. I loved you like the child I could never have. And it wasn't fair! *None of it*," she ranted, a crazed line of slug-like spittle bubbling over her stained, red lips. "Father left her virtually his entire estate – yours now, my dear boy – with just one property for me."

His mouth wide open, Peter gaped at his aunt with incredulity. "You *killed* my parents?!"

"Yes, I suppose I did," she whispered furtively. "As I said, I made them disappear… like my husband," she continued, eager to relate a further unshared secret. And there was a hideously warped pride in her candid revelation.

"Your husband? But surely, he died in his sleep – of natural causes; I recall how devastated you seemed."

"Yes, dear – *seemed*. Clive died in his sleep alright, with the help of a pillow over his face!" And there was a chilling passion to her words, almost as if she were bragging.

"Jesus! *Who are you*?!" cried Peter, his hand shaking irrepressibly.

"He *constantly* sought my attention, reassurance…" she resumed, disregarding his question, "my *love*! And I felt repulsed by him. What was I doing sharing a bed with this chalky old relic? So I made him disappear, and I was his only beneficiary, so I inherited his entire estate." And, fully gratified, she swallowed the remainder of her wine in one indulgent gulp. "How was the meal?" she asked.

"The meal? *The meal!*" he bellowed. "*I don't believe you*; you're a *monster.*"

"No, dear, I'm not a monster. I love you. It's you and me against the world. As always. We simply can't allow anything to get in our way now, can we?"

"But why didn't you tell me all this before?"

"It never really came up," she answered, casually collecting the plates and arranging them in the dishwasher. "Anyway, let's get back to Ava. I've put up with her for long enough, and you despise her, so we have to make a decision, and quickly."

"U… um… I don't think I can," he stuttered dumbfounded. "I just wanted her to suffer for running away; I didn't aim to *kill* her!"

"Shall I do it then? Leave it to me and I'll think of something, and you won't be implicated in any way – not, of course that I'd ever get caught." And she refilled her wine glass and sat down. "Remember, everyone's dispensable, Peter. Now, let's retire to the lounge, shall we?"

And he poured a large brandy and followed her, like the innocent, unquestioning child he had once been, and now, solely where his aunt was concerned, the malleable, subordinate adult he had become.

In trepidation, Ava tiptoed to the window, swiftly drawing the drape back a few inches, in order to check the catch, but it was locked. It was then that she glimpsed a car on the other side of the road – was it Jen's? However, on waving in a frantic bid to catch her attention, came the stark realisation that it couldn't possibly be. Jen thought she was in Cornwall.

At that very moment, a Toby jug on the sill, too long sheltered by the heavy curtain, chose, in kamikaze style, to hurl itself to the floor; and the thud, albeit muted due to the thick carpet, could still be heard. So now, all-the-more frantic in her efforts to alert she knew not who, Ava instinctively screamed out, pounding her fragile fists against the double-glazed, and therefore totally unyielding, glass. Alas, to no avail. Before she had time to process the course of events, Peter, having already been disturbed by the unexpected sound, sped furiously down the hallway, burst into the room and, in a frenzy of fury, lurched towards her, striking her full in the face.

"You conniving bitch!" he screamed. "Think you can escape me a second time, do you? Well, *do you*?"

Shakily picking herself up from the carpeted, now blood-stained, floor, Ava held her throbbing face and looked up at him, like a wounded deer shot by a pitiless hunter. Why couldn't she have made herself small enough, quiet enough, invisible enough not to be heard, seen, by this fierce and hostile foe?

Believing herself to be utterly doomed, she remained inert, though when Pam entered the room, on discerning her forbidding countenance, Ava inadvertently flinched.

"So, here we are again, Ava. What a lot of trouble you persist in causing us all. Peter, there's a sponge in the bathroom; she can wipe up her mess. And fetch a damp flannel too; we don't want her dripping blood everywhere."

And like an obeisant sheep, he concurred, returning after a few minutes with the requested items.

"Well, get to it, Ava. And I want that carpet pristine. Right now it disgusts me – a lot like your chaotic paintings, the drivelling, talentless renditions of a deranged mind. Oh… and, what have we here? The pills you secreted in the pillow seem to have escaped. You can't get past me, girl."

This said, she stepped towards the door. "Come, Peter."

And, like a brain-washed lapdog, he turned the key and followed his aunt to the kitchen.

"Think about what I said earlier, won't you."

He nodded his head.

"In the meantime, dose her up with more sleeping tablets – but ensure she swallows them this time. Focus Peter; it's all in the detail. I'll be watching a film if you want to join me."

"Y-yes, Aunt," he faltered. "I'll be in later." And tablets at the ready, he unlocked the door.

Without saying a word, he forced Ava to swallow them, roughly sticking his fingers in and around her mouth to double-check. Then he tossed the container in the drawer, lay her on the bed, switched the light off and locked the door. And Ava remained stone-still throughout the entire procedure, the sole movement being her terrified eyes flickering wildly from side to side.

The Attempted Rescue

Albeit dark, Jen had briefly glimpsed Ava by the window and now stood outside the solid door, unsure of what to do next. *Should she call the police?* Or just knock and go in? Apart from Peter and his aunt's acute rudeness, what else did she have to fear? She would simply say she had come to see Ava, to visit. But then what? She needed to get her out of there. And fast. Away from Peter's clutches. Away from his aunt. The burning question was how? She clearly hadn't thought it through.

Maybe he had planned an overnight stay? It certainly seemed that way, but it was plain that something was definitely amiss. What though? What was she dealing with here? Had they locked her friend up? Or was there an even more sinister agenda?

After considerable reflection, yet still having no concrete plan, Jen wrapped her fingers tightly around the brass knocker, pulled it towards her and let go. The sudden loud thwack of metal on wood made her jump impulsively and she took a deep breath to steady herself. And a modicum of relief, that this impromptu decision had been made, brushed over her, as she waited in the now-chilly air for the door to open – to what, she knew not.

After what seemed an age, footsteps could finally be heard approaching; and she stood tall and erect, ready to feign a confident, unintimidated posture.

Before long, the dour, frosty face of Pam came into view as she unlatched the heavy door, forcing it back as far as the security catch would allow. The vein on her neck pulsed as she glared at Jen with fierce loathing.

"Haven't you done enough?" she spat. "You're not welcome here. Please leave."

"I've come to see my friend. I believe Ava's here," replied Jen in the most assertive voice she could manage under the circumstances.

"Oh, you believe she's here, do you?" came the unpleasantly stern and authoritative reply. "Well, she is, but she's fast asleep after all the ill-advised disruption she's suffered over the last week – all down to you, I've been told!"

"I just need to make sure she has not been harmed," continued Jen, instantly regretting the potential folly of her words.

"*Harmed!*" rasped the seething woman. "What on earth do you mean, harmed? What do you take us for? Now, remove yourself from my property right away or I shall have to call the police."

"That might well be a good idea," replied Jen, quietly standing her ground, yet at the same time chiding herself for what was probably another unwise comment voiced without due forethought.

"What impertinence!" spouted Pam. "I'd like you to leave immediately."

"What's the matter, Aunt? Is everything OK?" came Peter's emotionless voice from the hallway.

"It's that awful friend of Ava's. Can you get rid of her, please?"

Peter shot an uneasy glance at Pam, before striding to the door and roughly releasing the catch.

"Ava's asleep," he hissed. "And you are *not* going to disturb her. Come back tomorrow if you must." And he closed the door in Jen's face, secured the latch and disappeared down the dark hall to pour himself yet another large brandy.

In Jen's Flat. Sweet Retreat

"Where've you been?" cried Isla. "I was so worried."

"It's all fine," consoled Jen, slowly taking off her shoes and perching on the sofa. "I'll be visiting Ava in the morning. She was asleep by the time I got to Pam's house, so Peter told me to come over tomorrow." She hoped she had sounded convincing. The last thing she wanted was for Isla to become even more distressed.

"Tomorrow? Can I come?"

"It's better I go alone for now. I'll bring Ava back to the flat as soon as possible. Everything'll be sorted out in no time, sweetheart, you'll see. You should try to get some sleep. Oh, did you phone Abbie?"

"Yes, I told her everything I knew. She tried to put on a brave face, but I could sense her anxiety."

Jen gently smoothed Isla's hair. "That's only natural. Let's make some hot milk with honey before we go to bed. We got this!" she grinned. "Sure as eggs is eggs!"

And Isla could not help but giggle.

*

"Why on earth did you say come back tomorrow? Ava's got a swollen face; she looks awful! Also, she'll be a nervous wreck," berated Pam.

"She's always a nervous wreck! I just thought Jen'd be suspicious otherwise, that's all. We'll wake Ava up early and make her say *she* took the sleeping tablets, bashed her face, and can't remember anything beyond that."

"I see little other choice now," grumbled Pam, polishing off the remains of a second bottle of wine.

*

The morning sun brought fresh hope as Jen pulled on a pair of jeans and a brightly coloured linen top, before hugging Isla and preparing to leave.

"Why don't you invite Emily?" she suggested. "You can go down to the café and order shakes and cakes! Now, they're *always* a great comforter. And having your friend over might help pass the time."

"Thanks, but I'm not in the right frame of mind, and anyway, Marmalade will keep me company."

"Fine, if you're sure. I don't know exactly when I'll be back, but I'll be as quick as I can."

"OK. Oh, and *bonne chance*."

Misgivings

As he lay sprawled untidily on the bed, Peter revisited his aunt's disturbing revelations in an attempt to fully process them. She had confessed to causing the deaths – *deaths* – of three people whom he thought were close to her. That made her a murderer... and she was now suggesting they cause a fourth to *disappear*. And he simply couldn't gauge how to receive this cacophony of self-proclaimed crimes, because they were crimes, weren't they? They were aberrant, perverse, nefarious; but why, then, did he feel almost desensitised? A little shocked, yes, but not shocked enough.

Twisted, diabolic divulgence, driven by a deranged mind, had surely fuelled his aunt's confessions, yet she had demonstrated no trace of insanity, or indeed remorse. Instead these past deeds had been presented so very calmly, proudly, as if they were personal triumphs – perhaps trophies, or laurel wreathes denoting victory, and a stifling disquiet engulfed him.

Who was she?

In the past, she had constantly reinforced the idea that he was better than everyone else, that no one was good enough, that no one should ever come between them. Yes, he had been force-fed these maxims from an early age.

Sitting upright now, he recalled her frightful rows with his parents, whom he couldn't remember very clearly. He only knew his mother had been blessed with soft skin and a gentle, yet firm voice. He vaguely recalled his aunt screaming at her, but nothing more.

Without fail, Pam had exuded determination; she was distant sometimes, yet strong. "*Your parents don't deserve you; but I do,*" she had declared with a dogged sneer and hypnotic glint in her eyes, and without question, he had soaked up her words like a sponge. Always.

Now he wasn't sure.

"*You despise her,*" she had jabbed, regarding Ava. But he didn't despise her. He married her, didn't he? And, "*Who cares about Isla?*" Well, surely *he* did. He just didn't know how to relate to either of them. "*Be in control, Peter, be the master,*" she had taught him. "*Everyone should obey you, Peter. Don't trust the world, don't rely on outsiders – it's just me and you… always.*" And he'd never doubted her. Ever.

Until now.

Wake Up, Ava

The dawn sky was stained with a bronze-yellow hue as Peter paced into Ava's room and pulled back the drapes. But an initial trickle of tenderness faded quickly, only to be replaced by a guilty, impotent indignation, causing him to wince as he viewed her sallow, gaunt form further weakened by a bruised, swollen cheek, which exposed his handiwork to the world, unveiling exactly who he was. And he held back the urge to strike her again.

"Ava, wake up!" he insisted, a sad irritation rising in his throat. Why wasn't she obeying him? "Jen's coming later," he coaxed, hoping this would persuade her to surface. "And we need to talk before that. Breakfast's in the kitchen."

But there was no response.

"Get up, Ava!" Surely the tablets should have worn off by now. "Get up, will you!"

He shook her roughly, but she remained still.

"Pam," he cried, a shrill urgency in his voice. "Pam, help me!"

And, after mere moments, she was there, assuming

a rigid, emotionless stance, her grim presence commanding the room.

"What on earth's the matter, Peter?"

"It's Ava, she won't wake up."

"Of course she won't. She's dosed up to the eyeballs. I told you I'd sort it, didn't I? Are you hungry? Breakfast is on the table. It's poached eggs on avocado toast, your favourite."

"*What?* W… what have you done!" he screamed. "What the hell have you done?"

"Crushed sleeping tablets in milk, dear boy. She was still semi-conscious in the early hours of the morning and drank it like a baby. We'll check on her in an hour or so and then phone an ambulance and act terribly concerned.

"The container is on the bed laced with her fingerprints for the sake of plausibility, so all good. They won't trace them back to me, or you, I made sure of that. Now, let's eat or the eggs will get cold." And with a self-assured gait, she strode into the kitchen, expecting her nephew to follow.

But Peter did not follow. Not this time. He fell to the floor and wept.

"Peter," called his aunt after several minutes' waiting. "Hurry up!"

"What have you done?" he howled, hauling himself up and raging into the kitchen like a petulant child. "I don't want this! You've gone too far."

"Please relax, Peter. She'll be fine but will need a stomach pump for sure. I'll phone for an ambulance shortly. Now eat your eggs."

"I don't understand. What the hell's going on?"

"I merely wanted to see your reaction. Test the waters. Maybe you like Ava more than I thought."

Peter plonked himself down on the hard wooden chair and covered his head with his hands.

"OK, let's get your story straight. Due to taking sleeping pills on an empty stomach, she had a dizzy spell and tumbled, thus bashing her face on the side cabinet. We heard her cry out, fetched her a compress – there's one on the eiderdown – and put her to bed. She must have woken up in the early hours and taken more pills as the container lay open on the covers. See, piece of cake.

"I'll phone the ambulance soon, so when Jen gets here, Ava will be in hospital, and from there, due to her overdose, we can get her readmitted to the sanatorium. And you're back in complete control. That's what you wanted, isn't it? – until you decide what to do with the woman long-term."

A short while later, Jen arrived, and after mechanically parking her car, crossing the road, knocking on the door, she waited nervously, quite unknowing, beyond a frosty welcome, of what to expect. But not in her worst nightmares could she have anticipated such a harrowing scenario.

Within seconds the shrill siren of the ambulance, screaming blue murder, cut through the cold air, prompting her to spin round with a swift jolt to discover its purpose and rule out any possible connection to her friend. However, as it screeched abruptly to a halt outside the grey-gravel garden (devoid of any plant life, bar a small daisy, bravely boring its way up through the ash-lead stones and into the light), Jen's eyes widened as she stared mutely over at the paramedic, before shooting a disbelieving, accusatory glance at Peter, who, with a contrite, drained look, had just opened the door.

The events of the next few minutes somehow trawled in slow motion yet flew with blistering celerity.

"Where is she?" And Jen barged past him and into the house. "What have you done to her?"

"She took an overdose and fell," came Peter's grave and resigned response, half to Jen, half to the paramedic. "We put her in the room on the left."

At the sight of her friend's wan complexion and grey-blue lips, Jen shuddered and rushed to her side.

"Ava, my darling, oh Ava," she whispered, shivering wildly as she stroked a body sucked dry of care.

Rapidly approaching from behind, the paramedic gently held Jen's shaking arms while easing her to the side. Ava's pulse was checked, and her heart listened to – each step executed with stellar efficiency.

"She's barely breathing, we need to get her on oxygen. Hang in there, Ava, you'll be fine," reassured the composed woman, just in case she could hear her. And, in the blink of an eye, a stretcher whooshed by, and Ava was lifted lightly on to it, and with swift urgency transported to the ambulance.

In frantic pursuit, Jen leapt onto a seat by her side, but Peter held back; that is, until Pam, appearing out of nowhere, dug him in the ribs and told him to follow them to the hospital.

"Make damn sure that floozy doesn't open her big mouth to all and sundry. Stay by Ava the whole time. Act concerned. I can come if you want."

"No, I'll go alone," he replied in a tired, defeated tone, as he swept up his car keys and disappeared through the front door.

"Remember, Peter. It's just you and me. Always…" uttered Pam to an empty space.

Anxious Hours

As Isla lay stretched out on the sofa, stroking Marmalade – who, untypical of most felines, had easily adapted to his new environs, now spreading himself over her stomach like a blanket – she heard a soft tap at the door.

"Hello? Isla, it's Chrissie."

Eager to learn the reason for the call, Isla bounced up, sending the now-disgruntled cat flying, before flinging open the door.

"Hi!" she exclaimed, on seeing the waitress. "Is everything OK?" And she tried, albeit unsuccessfully, to conceal her fears.

"Yes, all good," replied Chrissie, attempting to calm her. "I've just had a call from Jen, and she said to tell you she's with Ava and will be back late. All is fine. She made me promise to ensure you had lunch. So what do you fancy?"

"Just toast, please, and a coffee."

"OK, but let me scramble an egg to go on top."

"Fine. Thanks, Chrissie. Could you bring up some scraps for Marmalade as well, please?"

"Of course. Won't be long." And she disappeared downstairs.

*

Given that Ava was in intensive care, Jen had battled with herself over how much of the unfolding events to relate to Isla. She was loathe to cause any extra stress unnecessarily, and so, on balance, had decided to tell her all was fine for now, in the hope that shortly, all *would* indeed be fine.

Peter informed the doctors that his wife was suffering from depression, and had taken an overdose of sleeping pills, the exact quantity of which he was unsure. But Jen remained wholly unconvinced. Nothing added up; this latest scenario was highly suspicious. Ava had been happy with Abbie, and he had, after all, forced her to come back from Cornwall – where her mental health had been improving daily – to his aunt's, a woman whom Ava detested! And Peter was hardly a shoulder to cry on, given he had initiated the problem in the first place! She didn't trust either of them; his aunt was toxic, and so was he. So something was indisputably wrong, and she hoped Ava would, in time, be able to enlighten her.

And whispering, "Please wake up, darling," she gently clasped her friend's hand.

*

After nudging food from one side of her plate to the other, only managing to chew and swallow a sparrow's portion – unlike Marmalade, who greedily wolfed down a lion's share of leftover chicken – Isla decided to phone Emily. She had posted a sprinkling of brief texts, but it was not the same as hearing someone's voice; distraction was sorely needed from all the waiting and overthinking. So she returned to the sofa, instantly joined by the purring feline, and picked up her phone.

"*Oh, Isla,*" came her friend's relieved voice. "*It's great to hear from you, I was worried. Are you alright?*"

"*Hi, Ems. So sorry I haven't called earlier. It's been a harrowing weekend and I just feel like hibernating until all is back to normal, whatever the hell that is.*"

"*You poor thing. Shall I come over and tickle you until you beg for release? We could watch sitcoms and stuff, and pig out on popcorn – I'll bring some. What do you say?*"

"*Sounds wonderful. Just I'm not sure when Jen will ring again or if she'll bring Mum.*"

"*Look, what about I come round now, and make myself scarce when I need to. I can do subtle.*"

Isla laughed, despite herself, and it felt good, as if normality had returned for a hug.

"*Yeah, that'd be great. Thanks. See you soon.*"

"*On my way as we speak. Love you.*"

"*You too.*"

*

Why did Peter persist in hounding her? Jen sighed to herself. Everywhere she looked, there he was, it was positively creepy. But the crucial issue now was, naturally, Ava. The doctors had said her heart was weak and her breathing laboured; she was extremely frail and would remain in intensive care, in the hope there would be some evidence of improvement, but at this stage, they had been told, it could go either way.

"You should go home and get some sleep," the nurse had advised. "She's out for the count, so there's really no point in you staying. Of course, we'll phone if there are any changes during the night. Otherwise, come back in the morning."

And reluctantly, not without protestation on Jen's part, they had stridden in complete silence to the car park and driven their separate ways home.

When Jen let herself into the flat, the two girls were cuddled up on the settee in front of the TV, Isla fast asleep, which was not surprising, all things considered.

"Oh hi Jen, I… uh, was just leaving," said Emily, quietly disentangling herself, before making her way to the hall to fetch her coat.

"I'll ring for a taxi," whispered Jen. "Thanks for keeping Isla company."

"Oh that's OK," she replied, pulling on her shoes. "I was happy to."

After Emily had left, a deep frown set, in ridges, on Jen's forehead, as she perched on a pink-painted chair at the kitchen table and sipped a glass of wine.

"Poor Isla," she mused. "It's so hard on her."

Exhaustion, however, soon cradled her drowsy form and within minutes her head drooped onto her waiting arms, which leant on the Formica top, and her tired eyes gently closed.

*

On Peter's late return, his aunt, who had been waiting in an armchair, beady eyes fixed like lasers to the window, jumped up, with considerable vigour given the hour, to let him in.

And barely allowing enough time for walking through the door, she grabbed his arm and led him into the dark lounge, where, propped in a cobwebbed corner, a solitary lamp vainly attempted to distribute a warm light over the surrounding gloom.

"Well, what happened?" she questioned impatiently.

"Nothing," came his weary response. "She's in intensive care with an oxygen mask and some device for her heart, I don't know, a defibrillator or something."

"What are you doing *here*? Why aren't you still with her?"

"The nurse told us to come home. Ava's out cold and there would have been no point in staying."

"So *the friend* has gone home too?"

He nodded.

"Right. Have a drink and get to bed. You need to be back at the hospital at the crack of dawn to ensure *that woman* doesn't arrive before you."

Peter stared transfixed at a hand-painted, stoneware jug on the hearth – one of his aunt's decided favourites. And he yearned to smash it, hurl it with full force at her foul face, but instead he poured a whiskey, downed it in one, and bade her goodnight before retiring to the confines of his grey-walled room.

*

As morning sent stripy beads of orange light seeping through the slats of her pink blinds, Jen lifted her heavy head from the kitchen table, and, after a cavernous yawn, stroked her messy hair and stretched her arms skywards. It was then that she noticed Isla, a thick blanket draped round her slight shoulders.

"Where's Mum?" she asked quietly as she slouched in the kitchen doorway, rubbing sleep from her eyes.

"Firstly, sweetheart, she's safe," reassured Jen, taking a deep breath before continuing. "She took a few too many sleeping tablets but is being looked after *really well* at the hospital, and is in a stable condition." Here, she crossed her fingers behind her back. "And once we get her out of there, she'll be fighting fit in no time at all, just you wait and see."

"When can I visit?" she sighed, her sad eyes dull and body slumped.

"Give it a couple more days, darling, and I'll take you, I promise."

Without a word, Isla nodded, then disappeared into the lounge, lowered herself onto the settee and pulled the blanket over her head.

Peter's Confessions

Doubt and anger possessed Peter as he sat holding Ava's hand, mumbling to her sotto voce, seemingly oblivious of the poor woman's comatose state.

"…Pam killed my parents, Ava – messed with the brakes so they'd crash… my *mother* and *father* – her own *sister*. And Clive… I didn't know, Ava. I swear I didn't know. I love you; I want you back."

And, oh so tenderly, he kissed her soft cheek.

Seeing Peter's car, like an ugly reminder, in the car park, Jen hastily made a beeline for the ward, concerned at him being alone with Ava.

On arriving, the door was slightly ajar, so she nudged it open and there he was, perched on her friend's bed, mumbling to her. His muttering was muffled, requiring Jen to prick up her ears and strain to listen.

"Ava… it was her… the pills. I gave you some but… why did you have to make me angry? *Why?*"

A piercing shock drilled through her, and quiet as a mouse, she remained, rooted to the spot. The seconds crawled by like hours until eventually he resumed his disturbing monologue.

"I'm sorry I hit you, Ava, please forgive me. From now on I'll look after you, I promise – and protect you. You'll want for nothing. You'll belong to me Ava – like before. I won't let Pam harm you again. Please believe me." And he sobbed real tears, before adding: "But don't *ever* run away again."

As quiet as a graveyard, a cold shiver shrouding her, Jen silently turned. And she could have escaped to the safety of the ward had Isla not, at that precise moment, decided to text. The ping was so faint, yet enough. A drop in the ocean, yet enough for Peter to spin round and fix her in his gaze. Masking her inner disquiet, however, she willed herself to be as normal – sullen, sarcastic – it was imperative she be consistent.

"You still here?" she sneered as she strolled into the room, pretending she'd just arrived. "She's poorly enough; doesn't need *you* to make it worse. Can't you find someone else to bully?"

Peter stared at her. And he was still. Too still.

"*Hellooo!* Are you here or on planet Zong?" she asked. Usually he was so quick to take the bait. This didn't bode well.

After what seemed ages, he replied, a nagging strain in his voice. "She will wake up, won't she?"

Jen sighed. "Who knows, after what you and your evil aunt must have put her through!" Her heart was racing. Had she said too much? "I hope to goodness she does," she added hurriedly.

But it was too late.

"*What do you mean?*" he spat into the cold air.

"I just…"

"*What did you hear?*"

A dreadful pause ensued, like that which holds a rabbit in headlights before the crushing crunch of its demise.

"I didn't hear anything," she protested. "You're acting weird. Weirder than normal, and that's saying something."

"I know you. I know what you're capable of! Were you behind me – *listening*? *Did you hear what I said?*"

"Of course not!" The fierce drumming of her heart must surely be visible. "Hear what exactly?" she scoffed, a false bravado driving her words.

"I know you… *interfering* – always *there*, coming between me and Ava."

"You're pathetic, Peter."

"*I know you,*" he hissed. "Do you think I'm an *idiot*? You're a *liar!*" And it took a mere second for his heavy body to lunge and his hands to lock onto her throat like a vice.

A blade of terror now etched its dread onto her face; she lashed out, her fists pounding, but became enfeebled, debilitated as he hurled her against the wall. Her attempted scream fell silent, her airways choked in a stranglehold.

"You're h… hurting me," came a near-soundless rasp, as his huge hands tightened their grip.

"Shh." His voice, albeit a whisper, held a malevolent power, a brute force which entrapped her, rendering her deflated, like a discarded hand puppet.

"I can't breathe." A tiny plea.

"*You'll pay,*" he spat. "I'll *make* you pay – for *everything.*"

Meanwhile, a million miles away on the blanched-linen sheets, papery eyelids flickered, their rapid twitching like butterfly wings. A sound penetrated the semi-conscious stupor. A sound all-too familiar. The sound of him. And an inadvertent shiver, a stark alarm, flushed through her corpse-like body. She sensed anger. Yet she felt no pain. The pain was somewhere else. The anger too. Vicarious, but dangerous. She was numb, the pain raw. Muffled breaths. Rage. Terror. An energy nudged her, its urgency begging, imploring. And as another stifled gasp echoed from afar, her fragile fingers felt their way out of their torpor, edging silently to her side, creeping mutely to a small dangling box, where, with a strength she did not possess, Ava pressed the red button with all her might, before sliding back into sheer oblivion.

In a timely flash, brisk, sweeping footsteps, issuing from the main ward, brushed ever closer, and, once alerted, the felonious predator, relinquishing his grip without a moment's delay, charged out of the room and down the steel-grey corridor, barely contained rancour coursing through him as his shoes clicked stridently on the cold stone floor.

Pacing fiercely past the nurse's puzzled face, his brief nod of acknowledgement surfaced as a mere twitch before he dissolved into the distance; reappearing just minutes later in the newly chaotic reception, where swarms of bored, fidgety patients flicked fleetingly through yellowing magazines, or gazed vacantly into space, defeated in their tedious wait for delayed appointments.

Also hobbling by, nursing gaping gashes and blackberry-juice bruises, were the walking-wounded; some with bones horribly off-kilter or snapped clean in half like broken Pinocchios. Imbued, too, on this chaotic canvas were zombie-like inebriates contaminating the sterile air as they lolloped and concertinaed like coiled slinkies. A veritable maelstrom! Mindful of nothing, however, aside from the persistently screaming rage ringing in his ears, Peter marched out of the building and into his car.

"Please check Ava," cried Jen edgily, as the nurse rushed into the room. "Is she OK?"

"Stable," she reassured on checking the patient's pulse, and leaning calmly over her pale form, spoke in dulcet tones. "Ava, can you hear me? Could you blink for me, dear? Just to let me know you're in there."

But her distant drone drifted unheeded into the sanitised air, soon to be sucked through the recently scrubbed surface of cold, whitewashed walls.

"Her breathing is regular," informed the nurse, turning to face Jen. "But unfortunately, no response. Who rang the alarm?"

"Ava must have," came the hopeful reply. "I was pinned against the wall."

"Goodness!" exclaimed the nurse. "Are you OK? You look as white as a sheet. What on earth happened?"

"Peter attacked me. Grabbed me by the neck. When he heard you coming, he absented himself. Bloody typical!" she piped, regaining her prior anger.

"You know this needs to be reported, don't you." And

she handed Jen a glass of water. "Is your neck hurting?"

"Thanks," she replied, gratefully sipping the soothing liquid. "It's fine; very sore, but I'll live. And, yes, I shall be reporting him. Not just for what he's done to me, but… well, mostly for my friend." And with a deep sigh, she glanced over to the bed.

Nodding gently, the nurse returned to Ava's side, in a further attempt to rouse her.

"Ava, can you hear me? If you can, it's important you let me know, dear. Did you ring the alarm earlier? It's fine if you did, I just need to confirm."

And within seconds, the slightest twitch of an eyelid blinked once through a silent tear.

Seeking Absolution

Peter shuddered as he gazed through the windscreen's lens onto the empty, chewing gum-stained canvas of the car park. And hastily grabbing his phone from the lining of the glove box, he resolved to ring Pam. His fears had to be shared. Maybe not all, but most, at least, of what he'd done. She'd be on his side, he was sure. And recalling her words (mantra he'd followed throughout his childhood): *Don't rely on outsiders. It's just me and you. Always* – he dialled her number.

"*What's the latest, Peter?*" she asked, devoid of any perceptible emotion.

"*Pam, I… I think Jen overheard me talking.*" He was shaking as he spoke. "*I tried to… I don't know! I didn't… I pushed her against the wall… my hands were round her neck.*"

"*For heaven's sake, pull yourself together, Peter,*" replied his aunt, a cold distain, like a slap in the face, fuelling her response. "*Stop whimpering. I loathe whimperers.*"

But even though her scathing tone was no stranger, the old despondency seeped through his bones, and his body, like an undernourished dog, grew limp. And it was a while before he managed to catch his breath and continue.

"*I was angry.*" His reply was wooden. "*She was standing by the door listening.*"

"*Don't sulk,*" she snapped. "*Listening to what?*"

"*I told Ava I loved her – would protect her, like before – and…*"

"A*nd, what? What else?*" Her exasperation was rising to a daunting crescendo.

"*I apologised for hitting her.*"

"*What? Why on earth would you do that?*" There was a long pause before her cold words cut through the silence. "*What else did you say?*"

"*Nothing. Nothing else.*" A hard shell had grown around him, stifling any weakness. "*I think Jen may report me.*"

"*What have I always taught you?*" she rebuked. "*Discretion is paramount. Have you learnt nothing? I'm disappointed in you, Peter.*" And, that said, she hung up.

An impotent frustration, sadly all-too familiar, engulfed him. It was clear he could never speak of the day's events again. Never tell her anything. *Ever again.* And, with churning indignation swelling in his chest, he turned on the engine and drove away.

On arrival home, with no thoughts of Isla in his head, he twisted the key viciously in the lock, threw open the door and stumbled into the dark hallway, where he hurled himself on hard tiles and wailed – wailed like the wretched child he now was; and the embitterment of all the days, months, years, issued into the dusty, web-strewn corners, wafting up the steep stairway to his dismal, empty room. But Ava's little studio was locked now, and apart, and did not hear his sorrow.

When his hoarse, blubbering cries had eventually ebbed, he lovingly recalled the presence of vintage brandy in the dining room cabinet, and was drawn, without hesitation, into its grasp, allowing the soothing solution to slip like nectar down his thirsty throat. And sinking ever deeper into the soft folds of the soporific sofa, his miserable reality faded into darkness.

It was a good while later that Isla appeared at the dining room door to witness, as if from afar, her father's inert body, sprawled out, half on carpet, half settee, with the empty bottle, his sole companion, lying spent by his side.

And, technique perfected, she swiftly mounted the stairs two at a time, before thrusting clothes, books, and toiletries into her rucksack and tiptoeing soundlessly down, immune to the now stertorious rasping emanating from the sofa to the hallway. And disappearing through the front door, she closed it softly behind her.

It was only when sitting on the bus that Isla finally received Jen's response to her earlier text which had simply stated: *I'm going back to collect some clothes and stuff. Let me know how Mum is.*

Don't go! Jen had written. *Not now. Can I phone you?*

Am on bus to yours, call when I get back… unless… she's still stable, isn't she?

Yes, all good, Jen wrote, a huge sigh of relief sweeping over her. *Speak soon, sweetheart. Love you.*

U2.x

Take Heart

Driving back home, Jen felt relieved in the knowledge that the details of her assault had been recorded by the nurse, who had swiftly informed security, resulting in Peter being temporarily blocked from visiting Ava, pending further investigation. And given her friend was now conscious, she would be able to request no further visits from the man, which would serve as an extra surety.

As she opened the front door, and careful not to reveal her injury from earlier that day and cause yet further upset – she had wrapped a silk scarf subtly round the sprouting redness on her neck – she focused instead on practicalities, informing Isla of a business forum she was to attend on the following morning, while playfully adding, "However, if you want, I *could* drive you to the hospital afterwards."

"What?" replied Isla in disbelief.

"I think it's about time you visit your mum. She's frail, but conscious, and the nurse said she should be stronger after a sound night's sleep and agreed it would do her good to see you. If that's OK?"

"God, yes! More than OK! I thought this moment would never arrive." And Isla fell into the warm folds of the settee, clapping her hands together over and over like a gleeful monkey.

After a while, her gaze turned to Jen and with a playful grin she mouthed: *"Nice scarf."*

"Ha-ha!" came the feigned scoff. "Mock all you like. This is veritable core, my dear. Fashion houses will be embracing my unique vibe soon; you just wait and see."

"Wow… *core*! Impressive banter."

"But of course, darling. Totally *au courant*, that's me!"

"Sure. If you say so."

And, laughing out loud, which felt *so good*, Jen grabbed a cushion, and tossed it at Isla, who naturally tossed it back.

The next day saw Isla at the hospital with Ava, who, though very weak, was nevertheless able to muster a cheerful mien, which on seeing her daughter came effortlessly. And Isla recited some poetry and talked a little about the success of *Twelfth Night*. Sweet Retreat was also mentioned, and due praise awarded for the new line of delicious pecan pastries, which she urged her mother to try. And much to her delight, her enthusiastic, avid tones seemed to work, leaving Ava rested and relaxed.

"By the way, I'll be going to school tomorrow," she informed her. "But will visit afterwards."

"OK, darling. Have fun. I love you. Thank you for coming."

"That's fine. Love you too, Mum."

But even though Jen had used her day efficiently in contacting suppliers and spending a short time at the meeting, her mind had constantly returned to the assault. And in the afternoon, after having dropped Isla off, she found herself perched on a hideously uncomfortable, metal-framed chair in the reception of the local police station, where she waited for just under two hours before being seen.

"How may I help you?" eventually asked a young woman, apologising for the delay, as they sat down in a small, dun grey office.

"I don't really know how to start…" replied Jen.

Within minutes, however, she had found her tongue and her words rushed like rapids as she recounted what she had overheard Peter say, followed by details of his violent attack. A brief history of Ava's abuse was also provided, and her ongoing concerns for her friend's long-term safety voiced with a blast of emotion.

The police officer listened carefully before explaining that, as there had been no witnesses to the attacks, it might be harder to make anything stick, even with red marks on her neck, bruises on her friend's face and the nurse's report.

"He could well counteract your accusations and produce his own version of events, which may implicate you or your friend."

She did promise, however, to carry out some inquiries and keep her informed of the outcome. But, knowing Peter, Jen felt less than reassured.

Tormented

The next morning, an inadvertent shiver saw Peter tentatively return to the land of the living; and a jolting spasm, like the awakening of Frankenstein, eventually sparked his jelly legs into teetering unsteadily to the kitchen.

How could he have been so wrong about his aunt? he reflected with bitterness as he brutally shoved a week-old slice of bread into the toaster.

She hadn't loved him at all, merely relished possessing, manipulating, controlling him! A footing she had never managed to achieve with her sister. No! Because her sibling – *his mother* – had been popular, the perfect daughter, loved by all, favoured by her father – and plain, unexceptional Pam had lurked unheeded in a dark corner, staring enviously in on the daily praise, approval, attention afforded to her growing nemesis. And her occasional retaliation had only ever resulted in harsh punishments.

So her sad, longing eyes had, over the many years, begun to glint with wild, unbridled fury, until she burst out of her incarceration and – *snip* – fait accompli, she cut her sibling clean out of her life forever, before stealing the dead woman's child, the consolation prize for all her suffering.

He had been a mere pawn, a homeless pup, a plaything to remind her always of the devious ruse she had kept secret for all these years.

But why had she told him now? It made no sense. And would she really have killed Ava if he'd given his permission? She'd waited, though, hadn't she? Waited for *him* to decide. Might that mean she did love him after all? But this consideration, which aroused a smouldering yet dead sensation in his shaky form, was soon to be interrupted by a piercing pain in his stomach, and his wretched body, responding with a numb urgency, lumbered to the washroom, where he vomited vehemently into the bowl.

After a strong coffee and vowing he would sort things out once and for all, he picked up his car keys, floundered into the daylight, and forcibly pulled the front door to. Since returning to the house, he had not once entertained thoughts of Isla. Not once. Now, albeit fleetingly, her name nudged into his head. Maybe it was the sight of a police car, which had passed him at the end of the street, seemingly searching for a nearby address.

As he drove off into the distance, his head space was wired grey stripes, like malfunctioning radio waves. A painful storm of raging repression. Galloping torment. The betrayal of his aunt fell heavy like a stone, crushing him, smothering him. Ava's soft, small hand, watery smile, faded-green eyes; he adored her, yet despised her. Wanted to savage all that she loved because it got in the way: Jen. Her art. Isla. They got in the way. *She* got in the way! He didn't know how to love her. *He* called the shots! How dare she have her own ideas, her own dreams! How dare she question him! He was superior. Pam had said. "*Put her in her place, Peter, or she'll leave you. Expose her weaknesses and grind her strengths into the soil*," she had said, saliva lining her lips and vein pulsing.

Someone must pay, he screamed silently, his head loud, thrumming strings, like a discordant guitar. *Someone will!*

Bizarrely though, on approaching a nearby roundabout, his fuelled fury inexplicably waned, impelling him to spin suddenly full circle and head for home. Visiting his aunt, sitting at her table, ever seeking her approval? No. That was not what he wanted right now. He needed to be alone, behind closed doors, in his own house. And parking outside his local off-licence, he replenished his depleted stocks, loaded up the car and drove home.

Last Lesson in the Afternoon

"You have five minutes. Start!" projected the teacher, setting her timer with an authoritative air.

Twiddling pen, helicopter-like, between fingers, Isla reflected, until her thoughts were interrupted five minutes later, by the instruction to stop writing.

"Isla, could you start us off please? Come."

And attempting not to appear horribly self-conscious, Isla pushed her chair back in a faux-blasé manner, before striding overzealously to the front of the class, all eyes following her every move. Once facing her classmates' smiling faces, however, she relaxed a tad, took a breath and read:

"Cowering in the corner. Alone. Silent tears a testimony to her grief. The pain of a thousand others filled her heart – their suffering, embodied in her, was her own. They had not deserved to die. She held the weight of their sorrow, and hers, deep inside, as she curled up like a scared mouse. Cowering in the corner. Alone."

"Well done, Isla. Starts and ends with repetition of short sentences, as requested. Some effective evocation of emotions."

Task complete, Isla momentarily switched off, wondering where they would go when her mother came out of hospital. Maybe stay at Jen's? Who knew? How she longed for a simple, straightforward life. It would come, she reassured herself. In time, it would come.

"Next, we'll have Daniel please," announced the teacher, cutting through her thoughts.

A huge, clown-like beam appearing on his face, the child proudly scanned the room, delighted at having been put in the spotlight.

"Belongs in a kindergarten," murmured Isla with a disdainful click of the tongue.

"He always gets your attention though, doesn't he?" teased Emily. "Do you secretly fancy him?"

"Ha-ha. Funny joke, Ems. You deserve an Oscar," came the sarcastic reply.

"Do get a move on, Daniel," urged the teacher, tired irritation now creeping into her last-lesson-of-the-afternoon voice, as he dawdled up the aisle playing the fool.

"Can I start, Miss?" he giggled, having finally reached the front.

"Yes, *please do*," replied the teacher with an exasperated nod.

And, wide inappropriate grin, given the content of his piece, persisting on his lips, the boy read with exaggerated gusto.

"Andy was sad. He sat on the bench with his football in his hands. The football was punctured. Andy was sad."

"Thank you, Daniel. Good effort. You have demonstrated an understanding of the task set."

"Sounds like a page from *Janet and John*," whispered Isla. "It's an infant school reading book from the 1950s," she added, noting Emily's puzzlement. "My gran has some in her cupboard."

Emily giggled. "You have a hard heart, Isla Mills."

When the final bell rang, the teacher, salivating at the thought of spending her evening with a macaroni cheese ready meal and bottle of wine, exclaimed jubilantly: "Class dismissed!"

Taken in for Questioning

It was the next day when the police finally caught up with Peter, with thus far no inkling of the sorry specimen they would find inside the house; one who had been slumped on the sofa all day and night, downing copious amounts of whiskey, while staring through an old, black-and-white film to the blank wall behind, with glazed-over, cataract eyes.

The polite knocking, which gradually escalated into an assertive thud, before rising to a cacophonous crescendo of thunderous banging, eventually penetrated Peter's muted understanding that movement towards the front door was now non-negotiable; and in a wobbly haze he staggered through the dark hall, reaching unsteadily for the brass catch. Moments after, icy bursts of cold air caused an inadvertent shiver to course through him as he gazed at the uniformed officers standing stiffly on the threshold.

The taller of the two, on beholding the drunken spectacle, raised his eyes skywards and tutted. It was the other who was first to speak, in flat, albeit authoritative tones.

"Mr Mills?"

Peter nodded despondently.

"In response to charges of coercive behaviour, we'd like you to accompany us to the station, sir. We've some questions which need answering – after you've had a strong cup of coffee, that is."

And silently the cornered man nodded his head, grabbed his coat and in a state of confused subservience followed them, like a stray dog, to the car.

At the Police Station

"She attacked me first!" vociferated Peter, now regaining a state of outrage after two substantial cups of black coffee. "Tried to punch me in the mouth! I merely retaliated in self-defence. That hateful woman is an obnoxious—"

"Now, less of the anger, please, Mr Mills," cautioned the officer. "The disturbing accusations of physical and mental abuse come from four different sources; the most serious of all, however, are from Ava herself, who, feeling a lot stronger yesterday morning, was able, indeed eager, to speak of her ordeal."

A steely silence wafted through the bare room like a condemnatory mass hovering unforgivingly over the terrible truth, and he could find no words.

"We are also currently holding your aunt, Pamela Stein," the officer continued, "who has been accused, amongst other unacceptable behaviours, of menacing threats towards Ava; namely: *It's simple, we get rid of her.*

"Also, your admission of coercive crimes towards Ava, while the latter was in a comatose state in hospital, was overheard. The witness's recollections of these confessions are as follows: *It was her… the pills… I'm sorry I hit you, Ava, please forgive me… I won't let Pam harm you again.*

"So, as you can appreciate, Mr Mills, we have some extremely serious allegations to investigate."

Peter's now-ashen face was carved in stone, and this deathly pallor must have caused concern as the policeman asked if he wanted a glass of water.

"I need to throw up," came the hollow utterances. "Get me a bucket."

A Few Hours Earlier

Pam Takes Control

Seething inwardly yet demonstrating, as was her wont, a perfectly composed exterior, Pam, with the aplomb and bearing of a Hollywood star, eased herself gently into the police car, quietly acquiescing in the drive to the station. And once seated in the interview room, she answered all questions with faultless decorum.

Jen's allegations, regarding what she had overheard Peter say, were read out in an expressionless yet clear voice by an underpaid, overworked policewoman, and even though the vein on Pam's neck started to pulse, it was hidden by a chiffon scarf (scarves hide all manner of truths), and her voice did not waver.

She simply said: "These claims are false." And face exquisitely masking her true self, she stared overtly at the dispassionate officer, looking directly and unashamedly into her eyes; so much so that the latter was forced to briefly avert her gaze.

When Ava's allegations about being drugged and

overhearing the words *get rid of her* were aired, she simply said the girl had not been in the lounge for the best part of the evening but lay sleeping in the spare room, so must have been mistaken. And, indeed, if she'd wished to *get rid of* anything, it would have been that vile cat, Marmalade, which Peter constantly complained about.

So, to confirm for the records, had she drugged Ava?
No, absolutely not!
Had she used menacing threats?
Again, no.

"Given the child had refused to eat," continued Pam. Oh, where did she conjure up such mellifluous tones? "I merely offered the poor thing warm milk, which was readily accepted, before turning in for the night."

To the best of her knowledge, had her nephew drugged Ava?
She didn't know.
Had he struck her?
She couldn't say for sure.

"When I woke the next morning, I harboured no contemplations as to whether or not Peter had drugged, or punched, Ava – or indeed both; but, truth be known, he *was* prone to violent outbursts, even as a child." Here, she had paused for dramatic effect. "He is my nephew and I have always tried to protect him; so when he informed me Ava had taken some sleeping pills and later fallen, thus banging her head on a cupboard; given her poor mental health, I suppose I chose to believe his version of events, even though, in all honesty, I would not wholly rule out other, rather more unsavoury, scenarios. After all," recollected Pam, "Ava's sustained many injuries in the past, which he always insists have been accidents."

Under the table, she clenched her latest Versace handbag in a vice-like grip.

That would teach Peter to betray her!

Peter's Punishment

In the other room, an hour or so later, Peter's interrogation was going far less smoothly. Ava's gruelling catalogue of allegations were raked over with a fine toothcomb; accusations from Jen, Abbie and Isla also scrutinised. And after listening to the list of grievances against him, a vague trace of guilt could be detected in his brief admissions, coupled, however, with an instinctive rise in anger and indignation towards Ava.

So, had he committed these offences?
Mostly, yes.
Did he regret his actions?
He did. Several of the mentioned events, however, had seemed overly exaggerated.

But it was on hearing his aunt's condemnatory words repeated to him, that his visage took on an ugly glower.

"Sh… she said what?" he snarled, unable to further contain himself. "Why would she do that?" And bitter tears, drizzling in a directionless trail, dripped down his whiskey-red cheeks. "Why would she say that?!" he stormed, jumping to his feet, and hurling the chair to the floor.

"Now, let's not lose our temper, Mr Mills," came the stern reprimand. "Or we'll have to restrain you. Do you get angry often?"

"*No, I do not!*" His reply was adamant, his sobs sour, which further confirmed the accuracy of Pam's earlier comments.

"Are you sure about this?" enquired the inspector, nonchalantly swirling the remains of his coffee round the cardboard cup, before passing Peter a tissue from the dusty box; and the latter gesture of kindness, albeit tiny, was sufficient to excite a gush of suppressed torment, thus releasing an avalanche of denunciatory declamations.

"She... she murdered my parents – tampered with the brakes on their car! And... and killed her husband – suffocated him with a pillow! She wanted to *get rid of* Ava! That's right. Those were her very words – *get rid of her!* There, it's out! I've said it. *She's a murderer!*"

"Is she now?" The officer sighed deeply, slid back on his chair, and stretched his legs under the table. It was going to be a long day.

"Yes. And... and the milk was drugged. My Ava nearly died, and it would have been all Pam's fault."

"Mr Mills, I must remind you any untruths in your statement at this stage in the process, will be deemed in court as perverting the course of justice."

"But it's true, dammit. It's all true. She confessed to me – everything!"

"Did she indeed? That all seems very convenient."

"Convenient? But it's true! Why don't you believe

me?!" An exasperated, indeed desperate, look emerged on his bewildered countenance.

"Because your aunt mentioned your elasticity regarding the truth."

"What?"

"Said your version of events could not always be relied upon."

There was an impotent silence as Peter gasped incredulously at the calm officer, while further tears silently meandered, like lost runnels, over his chin, dropping unnoticed to his collar.

How could she do this to him? How could she!

"Mr Mills, you look pale; are you OK?"

Peter nodded limply.

"Good. Then we may continue. We have decided to release you on bail until the court hearing. During this time you are forbidden to have contact of any nature with Jennifer Jones, Abbie Swan, Isla Mills or, indeed, Ava Mills. Do you understand the terms of your bail?"

"Yes, Officer."

"Ensure you remain in your local area until the hearing. Is this clear?"

"Yes, Officer."

"And your sister—"

"Aunt."

"Your aunt has been released pending further enquiries."

A stooping, fractured form now, Peter crept silently to the door, down the corridor and out of the station into the open air.

Out of Hospital and Back to Jen's

Slouched on the settee in a relaxed row were the three women, with Marmalade rushing, in a wild whirl, from one to the other, in his element at the abundant choice of laps to snuggle into.

"It's just like old times," smiled Jen, looking from Ava to Isla. "Except better still, now there are three of us - four including Marmalade."

"Yes! And I'm over the moon that after all these years, I finally found the courage to make a statement," declared Ava.

"God, so am I! Took you long enough, but when the last straw shamefully presented itself, *you did it*, and that's the main thing."

"I did, didn't I! And what overwhelming relief I felt. Once I'd actually started talking, the words just tumbled out, as if I'd parachuted from a mountain top."

"OK. Wow! I'll have to try that," laughed Jen.

"And both of your statements were rock-solid," continued Ava happily. "Mum's too, which reminds me, I need to phone; it must have been strange giving hers online, but she did great. She'd also taken photos of the bruises incurred, which was a good shout. I do miss her. Maybe we could go to Cornwall sometime?"

"Mum," replied Isla. "Not so fast. We should stay here until all this is properly sorted."

"Isla's right. And you're hyper now, which is great; but you'll need time to start healing, so small steps."

Ava nodded. "Yes, you're right, of course. What was I thinking? Don't worry, I'll wait. Take my time." And, after a deep breath, she sipped her tea. "Thanks, Jen," she said, "for everything… and you, Isla. You rescued me. I appreciate you both so very much, you have no idea."

"Oh, I think we do," assured Jen, glancing contentedly at Ava. "The journey home has been a long one, but you got here in the end." And she winked at Isla. "Didn't I say: *we got this*?"

"Yes, you did," she agreed. "Several times!"

Pam's Untimely Visit

"Peter, it's me, Pam. Please let me in." The knocking was persistent, relentless. "I need to talk to you."

Gradually, he dragged himself from the sofa and trudged towards the door. Leaving it on the latch, he said dully: "You're not welcome here. Go home."

"Please can we talk?" implored his aunt. "I want to explain – and… and apologise for what I said."

"Bit late for that, don't you think?"

"Oh, let me in, will you. Hear me out. I was angry, that's why I reacted. Angry that you said those things."

"I didn't bloody know that *that woman* was listening, did I?"

"No, of course not. That's what I realised later when the heat of the situation had quelled."

"Did the police say anything else?" he asked, worried she might have heard his latest disclosures.

"Not a thing. Why?"

"Oh, nothing," he replied, breathing a sigh of relief.

"Come on, Peter, please let me in. It's chilly out here."

Reluctant yet curious, he undid the latch and pulled

open the door. Pam followed him into the lounge and perched on a nearby chair.

"Could I have a glass of wine? It'd be so much easier to talk then."

"I guess so. Wait, I'll get a bottle from the cellar. But this better be good."

He marched away from his aunt, his shoulders high; her pleas had given him a sense of empowerment and he thrived on this, like a lion basking in its glory.

Ten minutes passed. She waited, trying to remain patient. *Where on earth was he?* Until eventually, he surfaced, dusty bottle of vintage claret in his hand.

"Apologies for taking so long. I was searching out my choiciest Bordeaux – as a peace offering."

"What a sweet boy you are, Peter," enthused Pam with rare affection.

Slowly, sedately, he poured the claret into the two crystal glasses, where it was gracefully received; and swirling the blood-red liquid around until wine tears settled on the sides, he offered a toast.

"To us," he said.

"To us," she declared, raising her glass, and she peered into his eyes, "…just us," she continued. "Always you and me against the world."

The glasses clinked with surety, like prison keys.

"I love you, Peter," came her simple utterance. "We can get out of this. I know a way."

"Does this *way* involve murder?" A wry smirk appeared on his lips.

"No, of course not. And, with regard to that, I do hope my private revelations didn't shock you too much."

"No," he lied.

"You won't ever divulge them, will you, Peter?"

"Of course not." Another lie.

"It's our secret."

"Understood."

"Good." And she took a deep breath before continuing. "The business I wished to discuss involves a close client of mine, a barrister and specialist in the field of domestic violence. He has years of experience; if anyone can get you off the hook, it's him. What do you think?"

"She said some horrible things about me, Pam," he found himself blurting. "Ava… she said some *bad* things."

"I'm sure she did, dear. But don't dwell on that now. At least consider this option; we have one last chance to escape all these tedious complications and absolve you of any wrongdoing. What do you say, Peter?"

And he rushed into her arms and wept like a lost child.

"I'm sorry," he mumbled. "It may be too late." Was there remorse in his voice? "So sorry."

"As am I. But it's never too late; have faith, we can sort this out, you'll see."

"I'm just so very exhausted," he replied languidly. "I can't take any more in."

"Well, that's not at all surprising, given everything. I'll finish my wine and let you get some sleep. You'll feel better in the morning. I guess you can't come to my house?"

"No. I have to stay around here; it was one of the stipulations."

"Well, that's not a problem, I'll pop over tomorrow once I've made a phone call. So, you're sure then – about the barrister?"

"Yes, fine," muttered Peter, a dreadful vacancy now stripping his face of any colour. "You've convinced me, we'll do it."

"You won't regret it," she smiled, flicking her cashmere shawl over her shoulders, and tenderly picking up her red-leather handbag. "See you tomorrow."

If he flinched for a split second, as she jostled the car keys in her hand, it was barely perceptible. And with arm round her shoulders, he accompanied her to the drive, where she slid assuredly into her car and drove off into the distance, leaving him with now-watery eyes, which trailed her until all was darkness.

"Forgive me, Pam," he said, returning to the house and pouring more wine. "Forgive me." And wearily, he lifted his glass. "To my parents. May they rest in peace."

Hours later, Pam's car was discovered wrapped round an oak tree just off the dual carriageway. Yet even though part of the engine had caught fire on impact, it was still possible to detect the damaged breaks and pierced hose on the fuel tank.

When the police eventually arrived at Peter's house, he knew it was over. And his stoical yet broken mien was uncannily reminiscent of his boyhood.

"She had to pay," he explained, a raw numbness stealing through him. "For what she did, she had to pay."

And, with a sombre silence in his head, he was handcuffed and driven to the station.

News Travels Fast

Given the recent trauma, everyone jumped at the sound of the doorbell. Surely there weren't any new developments already? So who could it be? But when the solemn-faced police inspector entered the room, all eyes turned to him, and a keen chill was soon to fill the air at the gradual revelation of Pam's gruesome demise, filled by an audible gasp of incredulity from Ava on hearing Peter being named as the killer.

No in-depth details of the murder were provided, but they were told that sentencing would be imminent, given this was an open-and-shut case, due to Peter pleading guilty. And, after clarifying the process of ensuing judicial proceedings over a quick cup of sugary tea, the inspector bid the shell-shocked gathering goodbye, promising to keep them informed, and parted for the station.

A heavy silence shrouded the room, and it was several minutes before anyone deemed it apt to speak. A bewildered Ava uttered the first words.

"But I thought he idolised her? I don't understand," she said. "It makes no sense. No sense at all."

"Well, she obviously fell from grace at some point." Jen shrugged. "And it must have been a colossal fall, for him to bump her off like that."

"Yes – what a massive shock, I can hardly believe it," rejoined Ava after a short pause. "She seemed so *present*, *solid*… and now she's gone. Forever."

"Funny how things can change so drastically, isn't it. Who would have thought it?" Jen sipped her coffee half-heartedly.

"I expect the police will escort Dad to her funeral," mused Isla in a whisper. "That's what usually happens, isn't it? Although I think I've only seen it in films, come to that."

"You don't need to worry yourself, sweetheart," reassured Jen. "*We* won't be going and that's all that matters."

"He'll get at least fifteen years for what he did," remarked Ava.

"Yep, even more with the other charges added on, and those are the important ones," reflected Jen. "Let's hope he serves most of those years, 'cause often there are early release dates for good behaviour."

"True, but it should still be a long stretch. Are you OK, darling?" Ava turned to her daughter, concern wrinkling her forehead. "You look as if you're about to faint."

"I feel strange, almost sad," muttered Isla. "How can that be? Pam was *vile*." Yet still tears came to her eyes. "Dad will be all alone now. His aunt's dead and he hasn't got us anymore."

"That's down to him sweetheart."

"Oh, I know," she agreed quietly, "But… he's still my dad." And the tears fell. "I think I need to get some fresh air."

"OK. If you're sure," replied Ava gently. "Do you want company? Shall I come with you?"

"No, thanks. I'd rather be alone for a while. Such a lot's happened lately. I just need to properly process it all. I feel like the rug has been pulled from under me." And a silent shiver coursed through her as she reached for her coat.

"What you're feeling is completely understandable, darling. We'll both need time to adjust."

And, clicking open the latch, Isla offered her mother a faded glance before stepping out onto the stairwell and shutting the door behind her.

A very long time, Ava ruminated inwardly.

"But you'll get there," said Jen, reading her friend's mind. "I know you will."

Sentenced

It were as if Pam had held him in an emotional stranglehold, obsessively maligning any chance of happiness he might have had with another. She drew him to her like a moth to a flame; he was a victim, a helpless victim. Or was he? How could this possibly be – with all his anger and hatred, his cruelty, bullying and destruction? Yet it was true that now his aunt was no more, all feeling had drained away from him, leaving just an empty vessel, sucked dry of warped, all-consuming emotions. His irascible, waspish eyes had become as glass, his tense, minacious body, stone.

Ava never saw Peter again.

The divorce had been straightforward, and the money enough to purchase a derelict warehouse on the outskirts of London, which she lovingly restored, transforming the main area into a gallery and creating a small two-bedroomed flat for herself and Isla with the remainder of the somewhat substantial space.

Isla visited the prison just once. And when Peter glimpsed her, was she mistaken or did his eyes flicker fleetingly, where every other part of him seemed devoid of acknowledgement? He was no longer a part of her, though, just a mere shadow. Separate. A distant, hollow shell. He asked nothing – of her, of Ava. Nothing. He spoke of nothing; he showed no interest whatever. And, unable to dredge up conversation, she had lamentably resorted to an uneasy silence.

Pam had clearly been the love in his life, the twisted, toxic battery of his being; and now she was gone, he too was dead.

And Isla ran, ran, ran through the prison gates, ran to freedom. Away, away from him.

And as he watched her leave, did the word 'sorry' struggle through the high-hedged labyrinth of his mangled mind… did it ever escape the dark, defective maze and jump, exhausted, to the sunlight? Did it? Or was the desperate yet gravelly apology forever lost in the clamour and clatter of the echoing prison walls?

*

A brief coverage of the murder case, which also highlighted controlling, coercive behaviour (CCB) allegations, appeared on the national news. And the eyes of Amanda (the colleague Peter had once wronged), widened as she watched. The truth was out. Justice had been served. He had been punished. And knowing this, she could finally, after all these years, start to recover. Heal. Move on. And her face relaxed, a sigh of relief issuing from her now-upturned lips, as she retrieved the document she had oh so painstakingly prepared all those years ago, yet failed to hand over to the police;

anxious, in part, that their response to the attempted rape might well have mirrored the company's gross inaction, but largely due to her attacker's menacing words: *"You say anything about this, and I promise, I'll kill you."*

"Yes," she sighed, pulling on her coat; albeit belated, she would deliver her statement right away.

*

Peter was sentenced to twenty-five years for murder with intent and five years for coercive behaviour and acts of physical violence. Also, at a later date, and due to Amanda's belated statement, three years was added on for attempted rape. The minimum overall period of internment would be twenty years, dependent on good behaviour. He would be in prison for a very long time.

"The situation's almost surreal," mused Jen, as she gazed at the TV.

And Ava and Isla, even though they already knew the final verdict, still held hands, and stared motionlessly at the screen in front of them.

"We won," declared Jen. "He won't come near you again. Not ever. It's over. Relax, Ava. You're safe now. You both are."

"Thanks for rescuing me," she replied softly. "I'll never forget what you both went through. Not for as long as I live."

"By the way, did you let Abbie know?" asked Jen after a while. "It's just we've been so wrapped up in all this, I wasn't sure if you'd phoned."

"Don't worry. I told her, of course I did. When I said a minimum of twenty years with good behaviour, she was massively relieved. And I'm sure she watched the news as well. I promised we'd visit her during the next school break, but she said she'd rather come here."

"No one can keep away from my home made cakes," laughed Jen.

"Talking of which, let's go downstairs and sample the latest batch," said Ava, and Isla nodded avidly like a Churchill dog.

Several Years Later

'Escaping Entrapment.'
By Isla Mills

Beatrice had learnt, only now, to distance and ignore the malefic, spiteful beings whose sole purpose seemed to be to seek out and disturb the peace of others. These days she could shrug off their salt-sour, scorn-veiled mannerisms, icy expressions, alienate the festering venom crouching thirstily in wait behind their ugly utterances. She was able to deftly distance their 'like butter wouldn't melt' comments, laced with strychnine, which had once upon a time infected her innocent, open soul, stripped her of self-esteem and thrust her into a dark, dark corner... but not now...

...Yes, she could even stretch to generosity from her new standpoint of knowledge... of power!

But once upon a time...

Isla placed her pen on the table. She already envisaged sharing a strong affinity with her protagonist, Beatrice.

"But let's see where the story takes me," she mused. "It's therapy, after all. And the beauty is, I'm in charge."

"Absolutely," replied Jen, sipping a glass of wine. "Long may it continue!"

"Yes!" clapped Ava avidly, a brush of contentment colouring her cheeks. "I'll drink to that!"

Other Books by Vivien Varga

Marika

MARIKA is a captivating and fast-moving story which transports the reader through time: from past to present, childhood to adulthood; from peace to war and sorrow to happiness. Interwoven are the tales of a mother, BERTA, and her daughter, MARIKA.

A count chooses love of a commoner over status. After a tragic death we learn of the transportation of a baby from her mother in Hungary to grandparents in Austria and a privileged life awaiting her. Years later, in 1907, BERTA'S story starts shortly before her journey back to Hungary.

In 1929 we first meet MARIKA, a young child aged five, living on the family farm in Hungary. Her capers at school and exploits with friends and family draw us into her life there. Later, in her teenage years, we see sorrow strike with the tragic death of her mother. The narrative turns to wartime and a harrowing flight through occupied Hungary into Austria.

This story is an ever-evolving painting of life, through hardship and uncertainty to romance and hope. After marriage there follows a journey to England. But will MARIKA finally find peace and a new home?

READER REVIEWS
"A stunning debut novel."
"Beautifully crafted and highly relevant. A compulsive read."
"sensitively combines humour and sadness…thoroughly recommend."
(Available in paperback and on Kindle).

A Perfect Ending

These stories reach out: to embrace, beckon, invite!

Such diverse themes are ever-present to explore, relate to, empathise with, as you accompany characters on their personal journeys, and experience vicariously their struggles, hopes and dreams. Happy tales present idyllic lifestyles in Mediterranean settings, of love, adventure and self-discovery. Floating Romans occupy the sitting room; poltergeists disturb your serenity in an old, haunted house. Fulfilment, belonging and peace are found in an Art Gallery; and a perilous boat journey in turbulent waters will provide trepidation and suspense. The presence of animals creates harmony, healing; the isolation suffered due to mental health issues, as well as coping with speech disorders and bullying, will arouse your compassion.

It's all there in these fast-moving tales, which you can dip in and out of at your leisure.

READER REVIEWS
"A book to look out for."
"Clever, beautifully written tales."
"...totally enticing. Would definitely recommend."
(Available in paperback).

ABOUT THE AUTHOR

Vivien Varga has worked as an English and Drama teacher in Warwickshire and the West Midlands and lived for several years in Italy teaching English as a Foreign Language. She now spends her time writing and travelling. *Marika*, inspired by her mother's stories of her childhood and wartime experiences, is her first book; *A Perfect Ending and Other Stories*, a book of fast-moving tales on diverse themes, her second; with *Rescuing Ava*, a psychological thriller, being her third.